MIDNIGHT HEAT
Black Phoenix #2

SARAH GRIMM

ACKNOWLEDGEMENTS

In many ways this book was more challenging for me to write than any that came before it. Perhaps because life took over for a while and my writing fell by the wayside. It's tough, climbing back onto that writing horse and putting words on the page. Fighting against self-doubt and an innate fear that not only may readers have forgotten me, but my characters. Lucky for me, Dominic seems to be a character with 'sticking' power.

I need to say thank you to my husband, who has never doubted my ability to tell a good story. He may not read the genre, but he is darn proud to tell people about his wife's books.

A very special thank you goes out to Amy Lillard. Ames, I can honestly say this book would have been that much more difficult to write if you weren't always just an email or text away. Your ability to reassure me at my most panicked moments and willingness to read anything I send you no matter if you were facing a deadline of your own is worth more to me than gold. You'll never really know how much your friendship means to me. <3 you.

Thanks to my incredible Street Team, for everything you do. You are the best! And to the readers who read my books, whether you've been with me since the first one, or only just heard about me – thank you for allowing me to share my stories with you.

~ **Sarah**

Special acknowledgement goes to my street team member, Melissa Aguirre, for 'Dressing Dom' in his leathers. And also to Kathleen Grieve for helping me make my medical scenes more accurate. I fully admit to taking artistic license with a bit of it, so any inaccuracies are mine not hers.

CHAPTER ONE

"Forty-year-old male MVC victim," the medic shouted as he and his partner pushed the stretcher through the doors and into the emergency department. "SUV versus semi. SUV rolled multiple times before stopping to land on its passenger side."

Adrenaline surged through Dr. Rebecca Dahlman's system, revving her pulse, pushing away the fatigue of an overly long shift. It worked better than the half pot of coffee she'd already consumed.

"Upon arrival at the scene, patient was unresponsive. We were able to get the c-collar on him right away, but had to wait for the Jaws of Life to extricate."

Gown and gloves in place, Rebecca ran her gaze over the unconscious man strapped to the backboard with orange belts as they swung into room one and transferred him to the ER's gurney. Her team, already assembled in the trauma room, moved efficiently around the patient, cutting off his clothes with trauma shears, starting large bore IVs and getting vital signs.

The medic continued feeding her pertinent information as she began her assessment. "Blood pressure is one-twenty over seventy-five, pulse ninety-five. Pulse ox is one hundred percent on room air. Pupils—dilated, equal, and reactive."

The guy was a mess. Blood covered his face, soaked the left side of his head and shoulder of his shirt. He had a laceration on his left upper arm; deep enough to require sutures, and some bruises were already beginning to form at his left shoulder and right hip from the seatbelt doing its job of holding him in place. Even more troubling was the bruise forming on his right side, a sign of rib trauma. Ribs weren't the only common injuries from impact with the center console. The ones she couldn't see were what caused her the most concern.

"I want an ultrasound of the abdomen," Rebecca stated automatically as she shifted closer and listened to her patient's chest. Lungs clear, respirations even and non-labored, heart tones audible not muffled and no abnormal rhythm. Good, no internal chest trauma. She looped her stethoscope around her neck and leaned in, searching the man's scalp for head trauma. "Get me a cross-table C-spine, chest and pelvis x-ray. Draw a full trauma panel, type and cross, and a urine tox screen."

Karmen Williams, Rebecca's best friend and charge nurse for the night, pulled the man's wallet from the pile of clothes on the floor. "Rebecca."

Directly above his left ear Rebecca uncovered the source of all the blood. Pushing her fingers into his hair, she palpated the injury site. The wound immediately began to bleed again. "No skull fracture that I can detect."

"Rebecca."

"I'll want a CT scan of the head and neck."

"Rebecca." Karmen's voice was tight and pulled her attention. "It's Dominic."

For a moment, a heartbeat really, the words didn't make sense. Then, she looked closer at the lifeless man on the gurney. As if in slow motion, Rebecca dragged her gaze up the torso, locked it onto the face partially hidden behind long, blood-soaked black hair. Her breath snagged in her throat and she froze, the echo of her pulse beating in her ears. It was a struggle to keep her hand steady as she pushed his wavy hair away from his face and focused on his mouth, those lips, the bottom one slightly fuller than the top, the thin, straight nose.

"Stud," she whispered, her voice torn.

His eyes were closed, ringed in thick black lashes. Were they open they would be the color of the sky just after a cleansing rain.

Her world tilted.

No. It couldn't be. This wasn't him. Dominic didn't have a goatee or a scar across his right clavicle. Dominic wasn't in California, he was in

London. Safe in London.

Not unconscious and bleeding in the middle of her ER.

Rebecca lost focus as the room began to spin. She grabbed the side rail of the gurney to steady herself. *Dom. My God.* Her chest felt as if someone stood on it, forcing the last of the oxygen from her lungs.

"You know this man?" the medic on her right asked.

How could she ever forget? He'd haunted her, both asleep and awake, for nearly three years. She knew his scent, his wicked sense of humor. If he was conscious, he'd be giving her a hard time in that sexy damn voice of his. That he had calluses on his fingers that set her body on fire. Calluses from years of playing the bass, something he did even while asleep, tapping out a rhythm against her hip.

"Yes," she admitted without thought. Then she pulled her head out of the past and focused on the monumental task in front of her. "Has he regained consciousness?"

"No."

"Okay, I want a CT scan of his head and neck." Relying on her training to get her through this, she slid her hands over his extremities, continuing her head-to-toe assessment, trying her damnedest to remain detached. Pretending she didn't have intimate knowledge of the body beneath her palms.

"You said that already," one of the residents made the mistake of pointing out to her.

"Then make it happen!" she snapped.

The room erupted with a renewed flurry of activity and noise.

A hand settled on her shoulder, a small gesture of comfort. "It'll be all right," Karmen told her.

Rebecca wasn't certain whether she was referring to Dominic's accident or his sudden reappearance. At the moment, it didn't matter. Hands clenched, she drew a deep, steadying breath.

Her stomach twisted as she stared at the monitor, watched his heart beat out a steady, normal rhythm. He'd been unconscious for too long. Should she change the CT scan to an MRI? Should she do both? Second guessing herself was not usual. She didn't have to. She was good at what she did, exceptional. But that was when she didn't know her patient—intimately.

The door banged open, bringing an X-ray tech and a portable X-ray machine into the room. Rebecca shifted enough for her to pass, but not completely out of the way. She was too fixated on her patient's chest. She frowned, noting he was breathing much too fast. The monitor screamed an alarm as his heart rate jumped from the one-twenties to the one-sixties.

Her Tyvek gown snagged as she stepped closer, moving back in to get a better look at her patient. It helped to think of him as a patient, and not the man she once knew. Helped, right up until she discovered her gown wasn't snagged, but fisted in Dominic's hand. He groaned, then met her gaze with a touch of panic in his vivid blue eyes, as if he didn't understand where he was or how he'd gotten there.

She gave him a smile. "Welcome back. You've been in an accident, but everything's going to be okay."

He frowned, then shifted. His grip on her gown tightened, his body went taut. Unable to move his head because of the c-collar, his gaze left her to bounce around the room like a ping pong ball.

She placed a reassuring hand on his arm. Waking to this...it would terrify even the strongest man. "You're in the emergency room. You've been in an accident. I know you're frightened and in pain. There's a lot going on around you right now that you don't understand. You're going to be all right."

Not reassured, his entire body jerked. "Get me two milligrams of morphine," she said to her staff. The medicine would ease his pain and help keep him calm.

"Look at me." Rebecca leaned closer, until her face was directly above his. She dropped her voice a bit, lost the professional tone she always adopted when working and took on the one he

6

would recognize. "Dom, look at me." It was a moment before his gaze met hers. "I know this is confusing for you. It's noisy, there are people everywhere, but I need you to try and remain calm. I'll get the c-collar off you as soon as possible, I promise. Just hang on, okay? We're going to help you."

He closed his eyes for a good ten seconds then opened them. "Becca?" he said his voice low, rough and too damn familiar for comfort.

"Yes. Hang in there. We're working as fast as we can to find out the extent of your injuries. Do you recall what happened, what brought you here?"

He frowned, clenching his jaw in pain. "California?"

"The hospital," she corrected.

"Why am I in hospital?"

"You were in an accident. Do you remember the accident?"

"I was..." His brow furrowed. He blinked rapidly.

"Can't remember that, huh?" She pulled out her pen light and rechecked his pupil response.

His eyes squeezed closed on a moan. His body tensed; muscles flexing.

"Are you having sensitivity to light?"

"Yes."

"Any blurred vision or blind spots?"

"No."

"Do you have any pain?"

7

"Yes."

"Where? Where is your pain, Dominic?"

"My right side."

"Okay." With the bruising present, that didn't surprise her. "You don't remember the accident. Can you tell me your name?" Retrograde amnesia was common with a brain injury. A concussed person had trouble with new information, like what happened to them, but not old information, like their name. To most all the questions seemed silly, but they were a necessary part of evaluating the severity of his injury. "What's your name?"

"Dominic Parker Price."

Parker? "What day is it?"

"Sunday."

"What month is it?"

"March."

"What year?"

"This year," he replied, his tone a tad patronizing.

It made Rebecca smile. There, finally, was a sign of the man she knew. "I'm going to move out of the way and let the X-ray tech do her job now, okay? We're going to get a few films."

She stepped aside.

Dominic made a grab for her. "Becca? Where am I?"

His short term memory wasn't intact. Confusion was typical, normal for his injury. Still, she couldn't stop herself from smoothing his hair away from his face. "You're in the emergency room. You've been in a car accident."

"I don't have a car."

"An SUV."

"No."

"Dom—"

"Where's my phone?"

"I don't know." Most likely in Karmen's possession, along with the rest of his personal effects, but there was no way she was telling him that. The exact location of his phone was inconsequential. Of far greater importance was assessing the extent of his injuries.

"I need my phone. You need to call her. Shit. She's going to kill me for this."

"Who?"

"Isabeau. You need to call Isabeau."

****

Rebecca stared without focus at the lab report in front of her. She'd read it once already; hemoglobin normal, no drugs or alcohol in his system. His X-rays were good, too. No obvious fractures of the neck or spine. She knew all of this already and didn't need a few minutes to read through the reports.

She needed them to pull herself together.

As requested, Karmen had located Isabeau's number in the cell phone's contact list and placed a call to the woman. She was on her way. Rebecca didn't know how she felt about being minutes away from coming face to face with the new woman in Dominic's life. A woman important enough to him that she was the first person he'd asked to be notified. The only person.

Liar.

She knew exactly how she felt. A little pissed off, a little frustrated, and a whole lot devastated. Even after nearly three years she wasn't free from the drag of hurt that came when she thought of the last time she'd seen him. She'd confessed her love. He'd run. End of story.

Only, apparently, it wasn't. Dominic was back. Back in the states, back in California. The fact that this time, she was the one who wanted to run didn't escape her.

Damn it.

A few deep breaths helped. Gathering her courage, she pushed through the door into trauma one. On the gurney, which had been raised to a semi-upright position, Dominic lay on his back. As the door swung closed his gaze locked onto her. She did her best to remain unaffected as her pulse took off.

"Where did you run off to?" he demanded.

Ironic, given the direction of her thoughts. "Your X-rays show no broken bones. Blood looks good, too. We're just waiting for radiology to take you down for a CT scan." As she spoke she placed his chart next to the small sink at the far end of the room and took down a suture tray from the cabinet above. "Your abdominal ultrasound found bruising of your liver, but no tears, so that's good. The ribs...they're also bruised but not broken." She looked over at him. "I see someone cleaned you up." With a bit more care than normal. No doubt just for the chance to be near him.

He had that effect on women. Women of all ages swarmed around him. Not that she could blame them. To say he was good looking was an understatement. Dominic Price was truly delicious—physical perfection, with a British accent and a smile that could convince a woman to throw caution to the wind.

She would know. One smile from him and she'd not only taken him home, but in the back seat of her Chevy before they even made it out of the parking lot. Rebecca shook the memory loose. So not a place she needed to go right now. Not if she wanted her hands steady while she placed his sutures.

"You're not here to ask more questions, are you? I only just got that chattering nurse of yours to clear off."

She glanced over. He'd closed his eyes. "I only have a few routine questions."

"There is a God."

"Of course, once I'm done with you and you're taken upstairs for the night, another overly chatty nurse will make sure to rouse you every so often and ask you a series of questions. She'll have impeccable timing, usually arriving just after you've drifted to sleep."

"Fuck."

She grinned. "Still as articulate as ever, I see." He made a sound that could have been a laugh. She wasn't sure. "Do you have any allergies to medications?"

"No."

"Are you taking any daily medication?"

"No."

"Are you allergic to latex?"

He said nothing for a long, silent beat. "You know I'm not."

Her body reacted before she could school herself against it. Images flashed through her mind like a slideshow. They'd burned through more than a few condoms during their time together. Just the memory sent a burst of heat snapping along her nerves.

Commotion in the hall drew Rebecca's attention to the door in time to witness a petite woman storm in and skid to a stop. For a split second Rebecca wondered how she kept her balance in her knee high boots with four inch heels, but the thought was lost as the woman stepped to the gurney. She curled her right hand around the railing. "Dominic?"

She was young, mid-twenties maybe, and not what Rebecca would call beautiful. Concern colored her gray-blue eyes — really, very

12

interesting eyes. Pale, in a complexion that spoke of Native American heritage. Her hair was black, straight and hung to the middle of her back. A black leather jacket, belted at her waist, topped distressed denim jeans. The kind you paid lots of money for, not the kind you had in your closet for years.

Rebecca's patient opened his eyes. "Hey, Isabeau."

So, this was Dominic's Isabeau.

"Are you all right? How badly are you hurt?"

"I'm fine, luv. No worries."

She stroked Dominic's hair away from his face with a hand that trembled. "You scared the hell out of me, Dom."

"Scared hell out of me, too," he admitted softly.

Rebecca couldn't take her eyes off the pair. Specifically, the rock on the hand that continued to touch Dominic with a familiarity that made her chest ache. A princess cut diamond set in a simple platinum setting. At somewhere around four carats, it wasn't the biggest rock Rebecca'd seen, but with her petite frame, anything larger would have looked ridiculous on this woman. Instead it looked elegant. Particularly when paired with the equally impressive diamond eternity band next to it.

Dom was married?

She flicked her gaze to Dominic's left hand— his ringless left hand. He wore jewelry; his left ear was pierced, something she used to tease him about, and on his right index finger was a black tungsten band. When she'd known him, he'd also had a black leather cord bracelet he wore habitually. So why not a wedding ring? Especially when the set Isabeau wore was so well chosen, in size as well as statement. You couldn't look at that set and not know she was loved.

Acid burned a hole in Rebecca's stomach.

"Where's Noah? You didn't leave him behind did you?"

"No, I—"

"Leapt from the car before it was parked," the newest arrival in the room stated as he joined the woman at the gurney. Tall and lean, a build similar to Dominic's only a bit more muscular, with dark blond hair and green eyes: Dom's best friend and band mate, Noah Clark.

He hadn't changed much in the three years since she'd seen him. Well, except for his hair. The last time she'd seen Noah his hair had been shorter. Nowhere near long enough to brush the top of his shoulders, as it did now.

Rebecca frowned. The last time she'd seen Noah he'd held her as she sobbed, crying her eyes out over the same man who brought them together today.

"She's definitely a force to be reckoned with." Dominic laughed softly, then squeezed his eyes shut and groaned.

14

"Dom?" Isabeau asked.

"Bloody hell," he said cautiously, sounding pained. "My head feels like it's been run over by a truck."

Isabeau clenched the rail tighter. "You were run over by a truck."

"I was? Well, that would explain it."

The concerned expression slid off her face in exchange for a troubled one. "Don't you remember what happened to you?"

Dominic let out a slow, careful breath. "No."

Rebecca should have been concentrating on getting everything prepared, but she couldn't take her eyes off of the scene before her. Even though watching it unfold tore a hole inside of her. This woman, this tiny little thing, owned Dominic's heart. A heart she'd believed he would never give to a woman. She closed her eyes against the cold, hard reality. He'd been willing to give his heart to a woman, just not to her.

"Dom," Isabeau said softly, "you were broadsided by a semi. Luckily, it was the passenger side that took the hit."

"So your SUV is—"

"Totaled," Noah stated. A muscle ticced in his jaw. "It's still at the crash site, which we were unfortunate enough to drive past on the way in."

Isabeau shivered. Then the most interesting thing happened. Noah shifted, settled a hand on her lower back—his left hand. The move confused Rebecca, right up until she noticed a platinum wedding band on the ring finger of that hand.

What is this? She looked from Dominic to Isabeau and then to Noah. *Interesting.*

Isabeau might be comforting Dominic in a way that spoke of familiarity, but she was leaning into Noah in a way that spoke of something far more intimate. Dominic may have wanted Isabeau called, but she was not *his* Isabeau.

She was Noah's.

The tightness in her chest lessoned a degree.

"Damn, I'm sorry, Isabeau," Dominic said.

"No worries," she parroted.

The smallest smile crossed his lips. "At least you'll get to enjoy that new car smell again. I know how you like that."

"At six months old, my old car still had that new car smell."

His smile broadened, and he actually opened his eyes to look up at Isabeau. "About your SUV—"

"No one gives a shit about my SUV. All that matters is that you're okay."

"Did you just swear?"

"Dominic."

"I'm not sure I've ever heard you swear before."

"Dom…" Isabeau released a soft sigh. "You

are okay, aren't you? Dominic?"

He'd been clearly teasing Isabeau in order to distract her. Now his face was pale, clammy. With a groan he shifted. His breathing altered, his body went taut. "Shit," he rasped through his teeth as his smile faded.

"Dom?"

"I believe I'm going to be sick."

"I've got this." Rebecca grabbed an emesis basin from the cabinet at her back. She circled Dominic's visitors and placed the basin in his left hand. He groaned, gagged, but managed to keep his stomach contents in his stomach.

"Rebecca?" Noah's lips curved, but his eyes remained sober. "How are you?"

"I'm fine, and you? How have you been?" She broke eye contact with him to glance at his wife. "Really good I'm going to guess."

Isabeau smiled—the kind of friendly smile that had to be returned. "Isabeau Clark," she supplied. "We didn't mean to be rude. We didn't realize you were standing back there."

"Dr. Rebecca Dahlman, and don't worry about it. You were preoccupied."

"We were worried."

"I understand."

Isabeau's gaze slid over Dominic, and she frowned. "Can you tell me how he's doing? What is the extent of his injuries?"

"His X-rays are negative, no broken bones. His blood work is good. He's got a few

17

lacerations, multiple contusions, and a concussion. We'll be moving him up to the I.C.U in a bit, where we can monitor his hemoglobin levels and—"

"Hemoglobin levels?"

"Dominic has a bruised liver. We need to monitor his hemoglobin levels overnight."

"You mean he's bleeding..." Isabeau's eyes went a bit unfocused, her color faded to gray.

It wouldn't do to have this wisp of a woman pass out on her. "It's a relatively mild injury."

"But?"

She didn't miss much, did she? Rebecca believed she'd done an adequate job of hiding her misgivings. Apparently, she hadn't. She sighed, wishing like hell she could tell them something definitive, something to ease their worry, but she didn't have all the information yet. "My greatest concern is the head trauma. His test scores indicate a concussion, but dilated pupils and loss of consciousness for greater than thirty minutes usually indicate a more severe brain injury."

Isabeau reached over her shoulder and fisted her hand around Noah's jacket lapel. Noah covered his wife's hand with his own.

"I've ordered a CT scan. That should tell me what I need to know."

Noah stared at her. "Jesus," he finally said. "And if it's the more serious injury? Then what?"

"He's in a lot of pain, probably more than he

lets on, but he's doing really well," Rebecca reassured them, as well as herself. "He still doesn't recall the accident, but he understands where he is, so he's forming new memories. He can carry on a conversation and pieces of his personality are showing. That's a good thing, as severe traumatic brain injuries can cause personality changes. I'll know more when his CT scan is done."

Her color slightly improved, Isabeau swallowed. "How soon will that be?"

"I'm going to repair his lacerations. Then, if they still haven't come for him, I'll go see about expediting his scan."

"We'll be in the waiting room," Noah said.

"Sure."

Rebecca watched them go, Noah holding the door open for his wife, his hand settling on her lower back as he slipped out behind her.

CHAPTER TWO

Dominic couldn't recall the last time he hurt this damn bad. Which could mean one of two things: either he had a more serious injury than Rebecca was letting on, one that messed with his memories, or he'd never hurt this bad. For now, he was going to go with the latter.

He kept his eyes closed because he hurt less that way. At least with his eyes closed, his eyelids provided some barrier against the laser bore of the overhead lamp. He wished like hell he could turn it off, but Rebecca was there, preparing to sew him up and she needed the light.

Rebecca. Bloody hell. That he'd ended up in her hospital...he couldn't wrap his mind around it. What were the odds? They had to be astronomical.

He still couldn't recollect what had happened. The band had been in the recording studio, working on their first new album in ten years. It hadn't been going well because... His head throbbed in perfect harmony with his heartbeat. A wave of nausea washed over him and he tightened his hold on the little plastic basin.

Shit.

He recalled driving, racing down the interstate toward Sacramento. Thinking how he needed to get laid. Knowing it wasn't going to happen because he was in California. He hated this state. Hated the memories it evoked—the memories that pressed in on him no matter how fast he traveled.

Next thing he knew he awoke to a familiar voice barking out orders, demanding action. A voice edged with urgency and perhaps a tinge of fear. A voice that tugged at his memory.

"Dominic?"

Yeah, that voice.

"I'm going to repair the laceration on your bicep first. Dom?"

"Shhh." If she didn't stop yelling, his head was going to explode.

She went quiet, the only noise in the room the squeak of the stool she'd pulled up to the left side of the bed, and the ticking of the clock on the wall. Then there was a soft snick.

His head throbbed.

The cool swipe of something across his arm.

His stomach turned.

The bite of a needle sliding into his flesh.

He hissed out a breath. "Warn a man, will you?"

"You told me not to talk."

"Jesus."

21

"I'm going to inject the local anesthetic now. It might sting a bit."

"Yeah, I got that." He didn't even try to keep the annoyance out of his voice.

"Baby," Rebecca said under her breath as she stuck him again, then once more.

"Sadist."

She laughed softly and Dominic smiled. Then she ran her fingers through his hair, gently outlining the injury above his left ear and his smile faded. It should have hurt like hell. Instead, it made him ache. For the days when she touched him because she wanted to, not because it was her job.

Damn it, the past was a place he didn't want to visit tonight. Reliving the pain and loss didn't change anything. He'd hurt Becca too much to ever hope he would have a chance to make up for prior mistakes. He couldn't have her. Deep down in his gut he knew that. But it didn't ease the frustration. It didn't lessen the anguish inside of him.

"Do you have a preference to how I close this one?"

"You're the doctor."

"I'll glue it."

He grunted.

"So, you were driving Isabeau's car?"

"Her SUV. I prefer Noah's Aston Martin convertible, but...I don't remember why I was in the SUV."

"It'll come back to you. For now, be happy you were. After all, if you'd been in his convertible, that handsome face of yours would be a permanent fixture in a semi's grille."

He hadn't considered that.

"She was very worried when she got here. You were trying pretty hard to allay her fear. You must care deeply for her."

"Isabeau? I do." Like a sister. At least he thought the way be felt about her was comparable to the feelings one would have for a sister. He didn't have any siblings, so he didn't know if siblings got as close as he and Isabeau.

He'd never shared a friendship with a woman before. Never shared much with a woman beyond sex. Yet, with Isabeau it was different. She knew most of his secrets, and he knew most of hers. Like the demons she continued to struggle with after her own automobile accident years ago. "I'm sure it brought back a few painful memories for her."

"Her left hand?"

"You noticed her scars?"

"The rock caught my eye first. It definitely makes a statement."

"What statement is that?"

"It says taken in bold, capital letters."

He chuckled, then groaned when the action made his head throb, and his side scream. "Pretty sure that's what Noah was going for. He's a bit...enamored, with his wife."

23

There was the briefest hesitation before she replied, "At first I thought she was with you, that it was your statement."

He could have told her that Isabeau wasn't his type, that he liked his women to have more meat on their bones. Liked them full breasted, with enough ass to fill his hands. When he had a woman beneath him, he wanted to know that she could handle anything he gave her. He didn't want to have to worry she'd break. He could have told her that the last woman he'd been with had been everything and more than he wanted in a woman. And because of it he hadn't been with anyone since. Not in years.

Nearly three, to be exact.

He kept all of that to himself.

"Can you feel that?"

She meant the poke to his arm, not the ache of need that lodged in his chest. "Pressure. No pain."

"Good. How long have you been back in the States?"

"Ten months. Three in Long Island City, New York, the rest at Noah and Isabeau's in Auburn." With a deep breath in preparation of the assault his head was going to take, he opened his eyes. "I've been meaning to call you."

She glanced at him before refocusing on his arm. "I'm sure you have," she said, her tone disbelieving. "When was your last tetanus shot?"

"I have no idea."

"You'll need one." Rebecca held the needle away from his skin, picked up a pair of scissors, snipped, and placed everything on the tray at her right. "There you go, Stud, you won't even have a noticeable scar."

"I've always hated how you call me that."

"I know, but it fits you so well. You'll have to lose the jewelry, nothing metal near the CT scanner."

He removed the small hoop from his ear and the ring from his index finger, dropping them in the pocket of her lab coat when she held it open for him. "Give them to Isabeau."

"Sure." She scooped something off the tray, pushed his hair back with her left hand, and bent over him again. So close her hot breath brushed across his skin when she spoke. "I'm going to use tissue adhesive on this laceration. I've been told it stings like hell. You might also feel a small amount of heat as it dries."

She was right.

"Almost done here." She bent over him and a piece of her hair slid free from the intricate knot at the back of her neck, laying like fire across her cheek. He wanted to skim his fingertips over it. One touch. One touch he wanted so damn badly his hands began to shake.

Dominic dragged in air to loosen the knots in his stomach and only succeeded in filling his lungs with her scent. A scent he'd never quite

25

managed to forget. "Jesus, you smell good."

"Obviously, your olfactory system was damaged in that accident as I smell like I've been at this for sixteen hours already."

Then she looked down and the air between them thickened. A deep breath became impossible.

Three years. Three agonizingly long goddamn years. Because of him. Because she'd cared and that scared the hell out of him.

"I love you, Dominic."

Okay, she'd more than cared. God, he'd fucked up. If he hadn't been absolutely sure of that before, he was now. Laying here, her touching him as if he were nothing but another patient instead of the man she'd once confessed to love. Looking at him as if seeing him again was no big deal, as if it wasn't the giant kick in the ribs that seeing her again was for him.

She was coolly professional. Calm and unflustered. While he was..."I'm sorry, Becca."

She straightened away from him as if his words burned. Pushed to her feet so quickly the stool she'd been sitting on skidded backward and bounced off the wall.

The metallic clang echoed in Dominic's skull. Pain exploded behind his eyes. Nausea washed over him.

Rebecca opened her mouth to respond, then closed it and took a step in retreat. She removed her gloves, disposed of them and shut off the overhead lamp. Then she refocused on him and sighed. "Dominic, we..." She was quiet a moment, just looking at him and he held his breath. "I can't give you anything more for the pain until after the scan."

It was his turn to sigh. "It doesn't matter." There was nothing she could give him that would help.

Except for forgiveness. *Never gonna happen, mate.*

"Someone will come by soon and take you down for your CT scan."

Bloody wonderful. Dominic let out a breath. He forced himself to watch her leave. Walk away from him, the way he had done to her. He didn't need an expensive college degree to know he wasn't going to see her again. Not tonight. Not any time in the near future.

"Lights on or off?" she asked softly.

"Off."

She curled her hand around the door pull before plunging the room into darkness. Which was perfect, really, because he found he wasn't strong enough to watch her walk away after all.

****

Damn it. Damn it. *Damn it.*

Rebecca walked with purpose in the direction of the radiology department. She needed to make arrangements to have Dominic admitted for overnight observation. But before she could do that, she needed to see what the holdup was on his CT scan. The sooner she could get him scanned, the sooner she could get him upstairs, out of the emergency department, and her care. Then, she could escape home, crawl into bed, and put this night behind her.

Her emotions were in turmoil; had been since they'd wheeled him through those doors unconscious and bleeding. Damn, why did he still have to look so good? And why, oh why did he have to apologize? The Dom she knew would never have said he was sorry. He'd been cocky, confident, and sexy as hell but never apologetic. Not about his looks, his attitude, or even the women who flirted with him everywhere they went.

Rebecca could handle the old Dominic.

The heartbreaker.

The stud.

She wasn't sure how to handle this new Dominic.

Injured.

Vulnerable.

"Sorry doesn't cut it, Stud." But it was a start.

Damn him.

Rebecca shoved her hands in her lab coat pockets and hung a right. As her left hand brushed past the ink pen and touched on Dominic's ring, she closed her fist around it. Heart stuck in her throat, she closed her eyes and took a deep breath. Having been up for nearly thirty-six hours straight, she needed sleep. At least eight hours of deep, dreamless sleep. Only she'd bet her sleep was going to be anything but dreamless. Not with the way she kept recalling the past.

Opening her eyes, she pushed thoughts of sleep and Dominic aside. Across the room, heads close together in intimate conversation, stood Noah and Isabeau. Noah was holding his wife's hand, then he lifted it to his mouth, and pressed his lips into the center of her palm. Isabeau's eyes slid closed, she swayed a little closer to Noah.

A knot of envy lodged so firmly in Rebecca's throat that she found it hard to breathe. Swallowing, she fell back a step and turned toward the exit, her fist tightened around Dom's ring. She was in the waiting room, not radiology. She could find her way around this hospital blindfolded, so why had her feet brought her here? More importantly, why was she still standing there? She needed to head down to radiology, away from these people who only made her yearn for something she'd lost long ago.

"Doctor Dahlman?"

Damn.

"Doctor Dahlman?"

Because she had no other choice, Rebecca faced Isabeau, who came closer.

"Was there something you wanted to tell us? Do you have an update?" Isabeau asked.

"No, I'm sorry. I..." She sighed and wondered how to explain this. *I'm an idiot*? That might work. "Honestly, I'm not sure why I came to the waiting room. I meant to..."

"Do you need a minute to sit down? I'm sure it's been a shock seeing Dominic like that."

Rebecca stared at Isabeau, a little stunned. Did she know about her and Dominic's history? How much of it? "I'm fine. Just a little tired."

Isabeau pushed a lock of hair back from her face, behind one ear, and gave Rebecca a sympathetic smile. "I understand."

She couldn't possibly. Yet, as crazy as it seemed, there was something comforting in those two words. Rebecca let out a slow nod. She tightened her hand around the objects in her pocket, then pulled them out. "Dominic asked me to give these to you for safekeeping."

"Okay."

Suddenly, the very last thing she wanted was to give up Dominic's jewelry. It didn't make any sense. He'd left her, walked away without a backward glance. He'd stomped all over her heart and she wanted to hoard his jewelry like some love-starved child?

"I'm sorry, Becca."

So was she. Sorry she let him get to her. Again. She dropped the earring and ring into Isabeau's hand and took a step in retreat before

30

she could do something totally idiotic like snatch them back. "I have to go."

"Rebecca, is it all right if I call you Rebecca?"

"Sure."

"Rebecca, Noah and I are going to stay until we get the results of Dom's scan."

She took another step in retreat. "Sure, okay."

"I just want you to know that we'll be here," Isabeau said with a terrifying gentleness. "In case you decide you do need to sit down for a minute."

Damn. She did understand, after all.

Rebecca blinked to combat the sudden burning of her eyes. "Thank you," she whispered. Then she turned on her heel and fled.

CHAPTER THREE

Rebecca didn't need more than a glimpse out the peephole to recognize the man standing on her front step. The tall, leanly muscled body imbued with sex appeal; the black as midnight hair. "Dominic," she said as she opened the door.

He stood beneath the glow of the porch light in a blue long-sleeved button front shirt, cuffs rolled back to expose his forearms, dark sunglasses and low slung Levis. Not the type meant to be hidden beneath a suit coat, the shirt fit his slender body like it had been made for him, emphasizing his broad shoulders and chest, his flat stomach. He looked like the rock star he was—absolutely heart-stopping—and like the first moment she'd laid eyes on him, every cell in her body stood up and took notice.

A slow smile curved his lips. Did he know the effect he had on her? Probably did. He'd always had that confidence, that touch of arrogance.

Wait a minute.

Something was different about him. That confidence used to have a vein of cockiness running through it. Tonight, it seemed to be missing. Surprised, she looked him over, from the top of his head to his booted feet and back again. "You're supposed to be resting."

His smile vanished. "I can't sit around any longer. I'm ready to crawl out of my skin."

He'd been released from the hospital all of ten hours ago, nowhere near long enough for him to be crawling out of his skin. "How did you get here? Tell me you didn't drive."

"You never told me I couldn't drive."

"No, I just told you to rest. You knew what I meant."

"The insurance company gave Isabeau a rental until she gets her new car. I was restless and thought..."

"What? What did you think? Do you have any idea how dangerous—?" Rebecca let out a controlled breath and resisted calling him a damn idiot. Barely. "How bad is the headache?"

He frowned. "How do you know I have a headache?"

"The sunglasses after dark look is a bit much, even for you."

"I never realized just how bright streetlamps were," he muttered.

"If you're sensitive to noise or light, have symptoms such as headaches, nausea, or dizziness, you shouldn't be driving."

He didn't comment, just stood there, eyes hidden behind the dark lenses.

"I can't believe Isabeau let you drive her rental. Brave woman," she stated, then leaned

33

to the right to look past him. As she spotted the vehicle parked in her driveway, she couldn't hold back a snort of laughter.

"You did not just snort at me."

"It's a minivan."

"Believe me, I noticed."

Not just a minivan, a baby blue minivan. Another unladylike snort escaped.

"Isabeau claims it was all they had."

"I'll bet it just kills you to drive that," she managed as uncontrollable laughter began to bubble up and out of her.

"I think she did it on purpose to get back at me for totaling her car and scaring her."

"From stud to soccer mom in zero-point-four." Damn, she liked Isabeau already. "Can you feel the testosterone leaching out of your body with every mile?"

Judging by the tight set of his jaw, he didn't find it nearly as funny as she did. Rebecca lost the battle. She doubled over with laughter, straightening just in time to see a dark frown crease his forehead as he folded his arms over his chest.

"Are you done yet?"

"I'm sorry," she said, trying to go serious and not quite making it.

"Are you?"

She managed to stop laughing but couldn't wipe the smile off her face. "Not so much, no." Although she hadn't thought it possible, his scowl deepened. "What's the matter, crabby today?"

He let out a low, deep breath. "Apparently," he admitted, surprising her with his honesty.

Rebecca sobered. Tension radiated off him, pulling every part of his body tight. "How are you feeling?"

He fell silent and lifted a hand as if he meant to reach out and touch something—her perhaps.

She held her breath.

His hand fell to his side.

She sighed. "Well?"

"Well what?"

"How do you feel?"

"I feel great."

"The truth, Dominic, give me the courtesy of it, will you?"

"I feel like shit. Your laughing at me doesn't help."

His level of pain could be gauged by the way he held himself, and his careful indrawn breaths. The doctor in her wanted to reach out and comfort. The woman in her wanted to reach out for a completely different reason. She'd never had such an irresistible urge to touch anyone the way she wanted to touch him. It had been there right from the beginning, their first meeting, and was still just as strong now.

She fisted her hands to keep from acting on the impulse.

"Can I come in?"

Definitely not. Even injured and surly, he still emanated so damn much testosterone he made her teeth sweat. Her heart did a little flutter whether she wanted it to or not. "That's not a good idea."

"Have dinner with me." There was the arrogance that had been missing a few moments before. His tone wasn't commanding, but left no doubt in her mind that for him there was only one answer.

Too bad she couldn't give it. "I already ate."

"Tomorrow?"

"No."

His brow furrowed. "Why the bleedin' hell not? Are you involved with someone?"

"I'm not seeing anyone, no."

At her admission, he stepped closer, invading her space. Heat emanated off him, and although he did not touch her, she felt surrounded by him. "Take a drive with me?"

The low, soft timbre of his voice thrilled her, washed over her skin like a caress, and she fought a tremor. The heat of his body warmed her through her clothes. Wanting to step closer, to press against him and inhale his all too familiar scent, Rebecca stepped away. Physically distancing herself from him. She only wished emotional distance was as easily achieved. "Drive where?"

"Does it matter?"

Not really, since there was no way on earth

she was getting in a car with him tonight. Not when just the sight of him had her hormones standing at attention, one whiff of him, her body thrumming. Not after spending the entire day thinking about him.

Remembering.

Aching.

Did he still hurt over the loss of what could have been? Did he still dream of her, of them? Had he ever?

Dominic blew out a breath and shook his head, his frustration clear. "It's just a damn drive, Becca."

It was so much more. Acceptance would be the first crack in the barrier she'd built around her heart after he'd walked out. With only the smallest encouragement, he would stop by on a regular basis, invite her to spend time with him. Which would, even if she kept her wits about her and turned him down, lead to more heartache. Just seeing him again made her yearn. Spending time with him was not an option.

She didn't know why he was back in California. The why didn't matter. What mattered was that he would be gone again soon. Dominic Price wasn't the type to hang around. And she wasn't stupid enough to believe she could change him. "Dominic."

He let the silence hang between them a minute, then slowly straightened, and turned away. "Forget it."

She watched him for a few paces, his steps slow, a bit too carefully placed, as if the simple act of walking caused him pain. The memory of him immobilized, his face covered in blood flashed into her mind. Hot on its heels was the confusion and pain that had colored his gaze as he'd stared up at her from the ER gurney. Her stomach hollowed. "Dom, wait."

He stopped at the end of her walkway, and faced her. In the dim light she could just make out the tight set of his jaw.

"You shouldn't be driving."

"If anything happens, I take full responsibility for ignoring your advice. Your medical license is safe with me."

He turned back to the van, which pissed her off more than his comment. "Damnit!" She stepped off the front step, caught up, and placed herself in front of him.

An eyebrow arched over the top of his sunglasses. "What do you plan to do, drive me?"

"Yes."

"How will you get back home?"

She hadn't thought that far in advance. All she knew was that the very last place he should be this soon after his accident, was behind the wheel of a car.

"See you around, Becca." He left her standing there, staring at his retreating back as he circled the minivan and opened the driver's door.

Damn idiot. "I'm following you to make sure you get there."

"Do whatever you feel you have to do," he replied, his tone giving away how tired and pissed off he was. "I don't care."

Rebecca stalked back inside and grabbed her purse. Then she did exactly as she told him she would do: she followed him, all the way back to Auburn. Until he pulled into the driveway of a large two-story contemporary home nestled in the foothills, and parked in front of a three-car garage.

She remained in her car as he cut through the landscaping and made his way to the front door, used a key to let himself inside, and closed the door without a backward glance. Then she turned her car around and headed back to her empty condo, doing her best to deny that it was anything more than concern for his well-being that had driven her to follow him.

****

Laughter echoed from the opposite side of the door, surprising Rebecca as she rang the doorbell. A quick double check of the house numbers assured her she was at the right place. She'd been raised in this house so the chances of getting it wrong were slim, but in all the years she'd lived here, or in any of the years since, she'd never known laughter to be a part of it.

The door swung open, revealing her mother. Her dark auburn hair was natural—the bi-monthly trips to the salon used to keep the gray under control, not to change her natural color. The smile on her face was...while not unnatural, it was definitely something Rebecca didn't see often enough.

"Rebecca, sweetheart, it's so good to see you."

"It's good to see you, Mom."

"Come on in." She moved aside and made room.

"I can't stay long. I have another shift at the hospital." In fact, she'd just come off one shift and had planned on catching a few hours of sleep before the next one began. "Dad said it was important?"

Her mother's brow wrinkled. "When are you going to find a nice man to take care of you so you don't have to work so hard?"

"She doesn't need a man to take care of her, Camille."

"Thank you, Dad—"

"She needs to continue her schooling. If you specialized, Rebecca, you wouldn't need to put in so many hours."

Please, not tonight. Though why she thought tonight would be different from any other visit was a mystery.

Her mother led her into the kitchen, seemingly oblivious to the tension that always permeated the room whenever Rebecca and her father were together. "How is she ever going to give us grandbabies if she's working all the time?"

"Grandbabies require a husband, Camille."

"Exactly and how is she to find one with her hours?"

Why did they always speak of her as if she wasn't standing right next to them? Perhaps the better question was; what was with the sudden talk of grandchildren? "What's going on?"

"The hospital is full of suitable candidates; all she needs to do is open her eyes. Who knows, there might be one standing right in front of her this whole time." *Oh, shit, she knew where this was headed.* "A surgeon, like her father."

"Tell me you didn't."

"Didn't what, dear?" her mother asked.

The doorbell solidified Rebecca's suspicions. Her throat went tight as a combination of anger and disappointment surged. She turned to her father. "Really? That's what was so important?"

He didn't even blink. "Get the door, would you, Rebecca?"

She headed for the front door and pulled it open. "You've got to be kidding me."

"I'm sorry?" the man on the step asked.

"Nathan." Her father spoke from just behind her. "So glad you could make it."

Rebecca stared at the man with the sandy brown hair and hazel eyes who looked like he'd just stepped off the pages of *Gentleman's*

41

Quarterly. Dr. Nathan Connelly, chief trauma surgeon at her hospital and her father's obvious choice to sire his grandchildren.

She'd been set up.

"Rebecca, how are you?" Nathan placed a hand on her shoulder and bent at the waist. "It's good to see you outside of the hospital."

She tipped her head so his lips brushed her cheek. "Fine. Thank you."

"Do come in, Nathan," her father continued. "We were just sitting down to supper."

Her mother came out of the kitchen and embraced their guest. "Nathan, welcome."

"We were talking about Rebecca returning to school. Becoming a surgeon like she's always wanted."

It wasn't her dream to become a surgeon, but his dream for her. One he was never shy about vocalizing.

Nathan turned away from her father. A smile blossomed. "You're going back to school?"

"No, I'm not."

A frown tugged at her father's mouth. "You've had your fun, Rebecca Jane. It's time to get serious about your life."

"My fun?"

"In emergency medicine. It's time to do more, become more."

Now probably wasn't the time to tell him she was thinking about quitting medicine altogether. "Why don't you tell Nathan the truth, Dad?"

"I don't know what you mean."

"No?" Rebecca looked back to Nathan. "We weren't talking about schooling, we were talking about grandbabies. Specifically, who was going to father them."

"Rebecca Jane," her father warned.

The whole evening was a setup, starting with the talk of grandchildren. Was there any aspect of her life her father didn't feel the need to interfere with?

"Congratulations, Nathan. By your invite, I'm guessing you are Dad's choice for the job."

Her father's jaw tightened. A vein in his temple bulged. "Where are your manners, young lady?"

God, she was tired of this. Tired of never being good enough, never measuring up to what he expected of her. "Mother, I'm sorry, I…can't do this tonight."

Her mother's hands were clenched together so tightly her knuckles were white. "Rebecca—"

"I really need to get some rest before my next shift at the hospital."

Her mother closed her eyes, shook her head, then opened them again. Her father's frown deepened.

Nathan gently grasped her elbow. "I'll walk you out." Neither spoke until they reached her car, where she stopped and pressed her fingers against her burning eyes. "I'm sorry, Rebecca," he said, breaking the silence. "I assumed you knew I would be here tonight."

"It's not you, Nathan. It's just..."

She'd never been good enough. Nothing she'd done had ever been good enough for Richard Dahlman. Eighteen years under the same roof, thirty-four as his daughter, and never once could she recall a single word of praise or a gesture that showed he was pleased with her. Pleased with his daughter.

No, he always just pushed harder. Pushed her for more, to go further.

Rebecca opened her eyes and blinked to clear her vision. "He never lets up."

"He loves you."

He loved the fact that she was smart enough to excel at anything she'd ever attempted. He loved that she was the good daughter, who toed the line, ignoring her personal wants and desires in order to make him happy. Whether he loved *her*—the woman who suddenly felt suffocated by her life—she just wasn't certain. "He has my whole life planned out. I've known his plan for me since before I could talk."

"There was a time you didn't mind that I was a part of your father's plan."

There was a time he would have been exactly what she'd wanted. But that was before Dominic Price had come along. Before she was given a glimpse of happiness; a life that wasn't blood and bodily fluids 24/7. Something she hadn't even realized she wanted until he snatched it away from her when he left.

Rebecca had spent the last three years trying to forget. If not forget him, at least move past him. She'd even dated the man to her right.

And what a disaster that had been. Awkward and a bit...embarrassing. Oh, maybe not for Nathan, who wanted to give them another go. But the spark she knew could exist between two people, the heat and the fire; it wasn't there between them, no matter how he wished otherwise. She and Nathan—they made better friends than lovers.

"Rebecca?" Nathan touched her shoulder. "You drifted away for a minute there."

"I'm sorry. I'm just..." She didn't know what to say. He was a trauma surgeon. He got a thrill from late night disasters and heroic efforts to save someone's life against all odds. He lived for the adrenaline rush that came with holding a life in his hands and coming out the victor. He wouldn't understand her need for calm, or that the stress was becoming too much. There was no way to explain that the lure of something more never vanished. The memory of her time with Dominic – the nights filled with laughter and lovemaking – never faded. Until the gloss around her life, the life her father had pushed her into from early childhood, wore off. "It's been a long week. And I have another shift in a few hours."

Nathan stepped back, his expression going grim. "I hear he's back."

"Who's back?"

He raised an eyebrow.

She sighed. "What did you hear?"

"I heard about an accident victim the other night. One whose identity flustered you."

Of course he had. The hospital was a den of gossip, and any bit of news – whether real or imagined – could spread through every member of the staff fast enough to make teenage girls envious.

"How do you feel about that? The fact that he is back, I mean."

"Honestly? I don't know how I feel about it."

Nathan nodded, then glanced over his shoulder.

Rebecca looked, too, spotted her father standing on the front step, frowning. "I should go."

"I don't have to stay, you know. We could go to a nice restaurant. You look like you could use the fuel."

She stifled a laugh. "Thanks for noticing, but I think I'll pass."

"Rain check?"

She looked up into his hazel eyes and wished, not for the first time, that she could feel even a small portion of the sexual chemistry that she felt with Dominic. It would certainly simplify things. But there was nothing. Not even a low hum of attraction.

At least not on her part.

A sigh escaped her lips. "I'll get back to you on that, okay?"

CHAPTER FOUR

Dom hoped this second visit with Rebecca went better than the first. The first was a success in the show-her-he-was-still-a-sorry-sonofabitch department, which would have been bloody fantastic had that been his goal. Of course, it wasn't. No, he'd had just the opposite on his mind when he'd hauled his sorry ass out of bed and to her doorstep. Something that would improve her opinion of him. Not lower it.

No such luck. He'd been too cross; irritable and out of sorts. Crabby, she'd said.

Hell.

He'd struck out in such spectacular fashion it was embarrassing; failing to improve her opinion of him, to even get her to take a drive with him. How was he ever going to win her back if he couldn't even convince her to spend more than a few moments of time with him?

At least he'd made her laugh, even if it was at his expense. God, he loved her laugh. Rebecca laughed with her whole body, no holding back. Her eyes lit, her face softened, and she lost that careful, focused always-in-control demeanor. Years ago he'd excelled at getting her to lose control. Laughter was just one of the ways. The other made him hard just thinking about it.

Leaning against the crossover, which he had parked in a way that meant she couldn't leave until he moved, he watched the side door of the hospital. Waiting; to do better this time. To show her he wasn't the ornery man who'd stood on her porch. He'd been warned during discharge instructions his mood could turn foul, but he couldn't have imagined just how foul. Even he hadn't been able to stand himself lately.

At least he was still alive and in a position to redeem himself. He hurt like a bitch, his entire body aching, every muscle screaming in protest of the thrashing it had received when the SUV had rolled. But he was still alive, and in a better mood than the last two days.

The door swung open, pulling him from his thoughts. Eyes narrowed against the sun, even though he wore sunglasses with the darkest lenses he could find, Dominic tracked Rebecca as she made her way across the lot. Unlike anyone else he knew, Becca rarely wore jeans. Today, she'd donned black trousers that sat low on her waist, and a lightweight beige sweater, both fitted just enough to show off her lush feminine curves. Her blazing red hair was shiny and straight, pulled away from her face in one of those inside out ponytails, revealing every freckle that dotted her porcelain skin. Including the one on the corner of her mouth, a mouth that at one time marked his flesh with kisses, sighs, and soft, murmured words.

She came to a stop in front of him. "Dominic."

"Becca."

"What happened to the blue minivan?" She made a show of looking around, her emerald eyes sparking. "You didn't crash it, did you?"

"Funny."

She grinned and he couldn't help but grin back. Damn she was something. For the life of him, he couldn't figure out what she'd ever seen in him. She was whip smart, a genuine card-carrying member of Mensa. He was a musician who barely made it through school.

After a few moments, her smile faded away. "What are you doing here?"

"Waiting for you."

"How did you know I would be here? This isn't my normal shift," she reminded him.

No, her normal shift was noon to midnight, the same hours as his. "I was driving by, saw your car."

"And decided to wait on the off chance I might come strolling out any minute?" She crossed her arms and nailed him with a stare. "Try again, Stud."

Dominic grimaced and shook his head.

"What?"

"Do you have to call me that? Can't you think

of something else to call me?"

Very slowly, she arched an eyebrow. "You want me to come up with something else to call you. Do you really think that's a good idea?"

He suddenly thought it was the worst idea he'd had in a long time. Not that his new name wouldn't be accurate, most likely it would be spot on, he just wasn't ready to hear what she thought of him.

"Because if you really—"

"Forget I said anything."

Her lips curved in wry amusement. "I can't believe it bothers you so much. You do own a mirror? You must, or you couldn't keep that goatee so perfectly trimmed. When did you decide on that anyway?"

"You don't like it?" He would shave the damn thing off as soon as possible.

She stared at his mouth, then lifted her gaze to his. Her smile faded. Her eyes darkened.

He knew what that meant and couldn't have been more blindsided if she'd kneed him in the bollocks. "You do like it."

"It's…"

"It's…what?" Dom straightened away from the crossover and into her space. She was staring at his mouth again. He leaned in, just a little closer and something came alive between them. Her breathing quickened. His slowed. "Becca—"

She took a step back and shook her head.

51

"You had to come back, didn't you? And if that wasn't bad enough, you had to be better looking? I've put on ten pounds since you left, and you..." Her gaze moved over his face and body like she wanted to soak in every detail. "Look at you. Why the hell couldn't you have gotten fat or ugly or something?"

For a long moment he couldn't breathe as his blood thumped harder. "Clean living?"

She released a startled laugh. "Like you'd know clean living if it bit you on the ass."

True.

"An ass that appears to be even firmer than the last time I saw it."

Christ. She's killing me. He moved back into her space. "You can grab a handful if you'd like, so you'll know for certain."

Her smile faded. She stared at him a moment, then blew out a breath. "You're a real bastard, you know that?"

His lips curved. "I am."

"You say that as if it's a good thing."

"I suddenly get the feeling that it is." She had not yet told him to bugger off. She hadn't even backed away from him.

"It's not," she argued. "You're also—"

"A complete and utter tosser?"

Her flash of annoyance was impossible to miss. "Does that grin usually work?"

"Work?"

"Just because most women melt with one

grin doesn't mean I will. Don't make the mistake of thinking I am like most women."

"I wouldn't dream of it."

"I'm still irritated with you." She was and it made his smile grow. "Damnit. What do you want from me, Dominic?"

It was his turn for a beat of silence. He weighed the odds of her acceptance against his getting shot down. The chances of a yes were slim. He went for it anyway. "Share a coffee with me."

"That would be a big mistake."

"Why?"

She gave him a look.

"Come on, Becca," he said softly. "I've been waiting out here for forty-five minutes while you showered and changed. The sun is painfully bright, making my head throb all the more. Is a coffee really too much to ask?"

She narrowed her eyes. "How do you know I showered and changed?"

"You always shower and change after a shift."

"Okay, smart guy, how did you know I was working this shift?"

"I drove by your condo. When you weren't there I came here." *Because that didn't make him sound like a stalker or anything.*

"And?"

"I went inside, spoke with the chatterbox from the night of my accident. I told her I wanted to thank you for what you'd done for me. She told me when your shift would be over."

"You don't even find that strange, do you? That people tell you anything you want to know?" The sigh she released sounded like exasperation. "She was probably hoping that after you thanked me, you'd stick around to thank her."

Judging by the tight set of her mouth, she wasn't too happy about the idea. "Becca—"

She held up her hand and shook her head. "Look, I worked two back-to-back shifts, with just enough time between them to attempt to have dinner with my parents. I've consumed more caffeine than most people average in a week, and I'm still so physically and emotionally drained that I've already lost the ability to filter my speech. If I don't get some sleep soon, I'll start rambling worse than I already am. You remember how I get."

He did. The more tired she was, the faster her mouth moved, usually letting loose something she would never have said if she weren't so vulnerable.

"Listen, I can't... I'm not going to share a coffee with you."

It was clear by the lines of fatigue around her eyes that she needed rest, but that didn't stop him from tempting her with the one thing he knew she found impossible to resist. "Okay, we'll do ice cream instead."

Her eyes went wide. "What? How is that better?"

"Strawberry ice cream."

A look of longing crossed her face. It figured he would finally see that look again and it had absolutely nothing to do with him. "I love strawberry ice cream."

"I remember."

"What's with the crossover?"

It took a moment to adjust to the abrupt change of topic—another thing she did a lot of when tired. Dom turned and focused on the vehicle under discussion. "*Luxury* crossover or so the salesman kept reminding me. It's Isabeau's new ride. I picked it up for her."

"Wow, three days. That's got to be the fastest insurance company I've ever heard of."

"The insurance company had nothing to do with it. They've yet to decide whether they'll be replacing her vehicle or not."

"What? Why?"

"Too many losses in too short a time frame."

"Can they do that?"

He shrugged.

Rebecca moved past him to the other side of the crossover. "It's nice. I love the color, more of a candy apple red than a standard red, isn't it?" She kept circling as if she didn't expect an answer, until she'd circled the entire thing and once again stood at his side. "Did you buy it for her?"

"Isabeau picked it out. She doesn't know it yet, but yes, I paid for it." She wouldn't be pleased when she found out, either, but it was the least he could do. After all, he was the reason she needed a new car in the first place. "Are you ready?"

"For?"

"Ice cream, remember? I'll let you drive."

"I can't."

"Sure you can. Everyone likes driving new cars." He certainly did. He had a lifelong affection for cars, especially sports cars. An affection made stronger by the fact that he'd grown up shit poor. The bastard son of a junkie. The scrawny, sickly loner who never fit in.

Until he'd discovered music.

He had a natural aptitude for the bass, a talent that had quickly turned his life around. In no time he became a common household name; no longer needing to worry about whether he could afford a new pair of shoes or where his next hot meal would come from. It had all been so new, so shocking that on Black Phoenix's first world tour, the one thing he'd done in every new city was slip away and take a car on a test drive. Fancy, outrageously expensive cars that as a young boy had been nothing more than a fantasy, but as a man could be a reality.

Could be. If he'd ever bought one.

But he never did, just touched them, reveled in the fact that he could own one—hell, five—if he so desired. Soaked up the way the stuffed-shirts tripped over themselves to assist him, instead of turning up their noses and taking a wide berth around him, or kicking him out.

For years it had been his guilty pleasure. A sad statement about his person. Bloody pathetic, really.

"Come on, you know you want to, Bec. It's pretty loaded. Upgraded audio system, voice activated navi. Isabeau doesn't skimp when it comes to her cars, although her love of SUVs has me flummoxed."

"It's a luxury crossover," Becca corrected, her voice full of humor.

"How could I forget? At least this has more horsepower than her Navigator, so it's more fun to drive. Twin turbos and a direct inject system that means it's good for the environment." Had he really just said that? Since when did he give a piss about a car's environmental impact? Performance is what counted. Speed and handling. "Damn state. I'm even beginning to talk like one of you."

"God forbid," she replied, then pulled the driver's door open and climbed in for a closer look. "Don't worry. You'll be out of this state in no time."

"Why do you say that?"

"Because you don't ever stay in one place long."

Not often, no. But he was looking to change.

"I'll be here at least another year." Her eyes met his and he wished he could read her, but couldn't.

"Here? In California?"

"Yes."

"Then what, back to London?"

Nope, still no clue what she was thinking. He'd give just about anything to know what was going on in her head right now. "Off on a world tour."

"With Black Phoenix?"

"We're cutting a new album now. Noah had a basement recording studio put in after he bought his house."

She was touching everything; flipping the visors, pushing the buttons that controlled the glass roof, and caressing the leather seats. Resting his forearms on the roof, he leaned in the open door, into her space. "Place your foot on the brake and push the button."

"Which button?"

He leaned in a little further, stretched his left arm over the top of the steering column until the tips of his fingers touched the button in question. "Is your foot on the brake?" Silence. He turned his head and discovered her eyes tightly closed. "Becca?"

"Yeah, yes, my foot's on the brake." Her voice was tight and a bit panicked.

Dom pushed the button. The vehicle started.

Rebecca's eyes snapped open. "Very nice,"

she murmured, her lips so dangerously close to his their breath combined.

Mouth dry, he swallowed, wishing he had the right to kiss her. Wishing he had the right to do a lot more than that. He remembered all too well the feel of her lips against his, sliding lower, down his chest, his abdomen…

Fuck.

"Dominic?"

He allowed himself a moment to absorb the memory, then pushed it brutally aside. "Now the one above you again."

She shot him a look that was a little bit bafflement, a little bit something he couldn't name. Then she pressed the button. The front glass roof panel moved and so did he. As the glass slid open, Dom eased back, replacing his forearms on the roof, he peered down at her. "Now that would get me in trouble," she said, squinting at the sky above her.

"Why?"

"I love the sun. I'd want it open all the time, but my pale skin couldn't handle it. I don't need any more freckles."

"I like your freckles." He used to trace them with his fingers, his tongue. Once he'd even tried to count them all, quickly becoming distracted by the woman they decorated.

She wrinkled her freckled nose and he smiled. Those were nice, but the ones dusting her breasts were his favorite.

"Buckle up." Stepping back, he closed the driver's door then circled around to his door before she could change her mind. Turned out, he needn't have worried. She didn't even try to tell him what a mistake it was, just put the vehicle in gear and headed for the lot exit.

The minute they pulled into traffic and Rebecca closed the glass roof, Dominic realized the severity of his error. Sure, he was a lucky bastard to be spending time with her in any capacity, but the car had been a tactical error. Now he was trapped, with no escape from the combined scent of new leather and soft female that flooded his senses. No way to ignore the way the sunlight slanted over her hair, hair he used to love to have draped across his body.

He looked at her for a long beat, her heart-shaped face, high cheekbones and narrow chin. Her full lips, slicked with something that made them appear soft and shiny. His pulse picked up speed. To counteract it, he closed his eyes and leaned his head back against the headrest.

"You're very quiet all of a sudden," she said softly, her voice shattering any hope for a few minutes to pull himself together. "Which is rare for you."

He didn't reply. He was too busy running mathematical equations through his head.

Too bad he'd never been any damn good at math.

"As rare as the fact that there's no music

playing. You know, from the upgraded audio system you made a point to mention?"

He took a deep breath, tipped his head and looked over at her. "You're not going to yell at me again, are you?"

"I don't yell."

"Right."

Her lips thinned to a tight line. "If I yelled at you it was because I was worried."

Suddenly, he felt a whole lot better. If she was worried about him it meant she still cared. His euphoria was short-lived.

"I worry about all of my patients. Especially the ones who are too stubborn to follow my instructions."

"I'm fine, Rebecca."

"Are you? How long can you keep your eyes open and tolerate the light?" She arched an eyebrow, daring him to admit the truth.

"With or without the shades?"

"Damn it, Dom." She glanced at him, her eyes narrowed. "What about the music?"

He let out a breath. "I can't stand to listen to it yet." This was disconcerting enough, without the fact that it was the bass that bothered him the most. For the exact reason he normally loved it. "My heartbeat syncs with the beat, then pounds through my skull. Instead of making me feel more alive, it makes me want to—"

"Cry?"

He'd been about to say vomit, because when his head really began to pound, that was usually the end result.

"So, no studio time, either?"

"No."

"I'm sorry," she said quietly, then turned her head and met his gaze, allowing him to see she meant it.

He felt a little thunderstruck. A feeling he wasn't sure what to do with at that moment. "It's not your fault."

"No, but it must be difficult for you."

It was hell. It had only been three short days and already Dom couldn't stand it. Music was everything to him, one of the few things he excelled at. He couldn't imagine a life without music. How the hell had Noah done it, given music up for all those years? He would surely have gone mad.

"So, how are you spending your free time?"

Thinking about you. Something, since seeing her again, he found impossible not to do.

Rebecca pulled into the Dairy Mart and parked in front of a picnic table at the far end of the lot, angling the car so the bright afternoon sun was at their back. "How do your ribs feel?" She pushed the sleeve of his tee up and ran a finger over his sutures. "Your laceration is healing nicely."

"My ribs are a bit troubling."

"You're keeping them wrapped?"

The gentle sweep of her thumb back and forth across his bicep was driving him to distraction. He'd bet she didn't even realize she was doing it.

"Dominic?"

Deciding escape was his best course of action, he pushed the door open and stepped out. The Dairy Mart had its fair share of mature palm trees providing enough pockets of shade so that his trek for ice cream was relatively painless.

The walk back to the picnic table was slightly more challenging as he was walking into the sun. The glare was uncomfortable enough that he was at the picnic table before he noted Rebecca sat atop it, leaned back on her elbows, copper hair glinting. Head tipped to the sky, eyes closed, her breasts offered up like a sacrifice to the gods...

Dominic stood frozen, unable to avert his gaze. It was a moment before he found his voice. "Becca?"

She raised a hand to her forehead, shielding her eyes. A warm smile lit her face, stealing his breath. "Two scoops?" She straightened and took the cone from him as he sat next to her. A sweep of her tongue around the base of the bottom scoop was immediately followed by a soft moan of approval. Heat flushed through him. "There goes my diet."

"You're dieting? What the hell for?"

SARAH GRIMM

He couldn't take his eyes off her. Who knew watching her eat would be so titillating? He wanted to touch her so damn bad. Wanted to lay her down on the picnic table, strip her clothes off and fill his hands with her amazing breasts. Kiss her senseless, then take his mouth on a journey of rediscovery, exploring every dip and curve of her body before rolling her atop him and letting her return the favor.

As if she would ever let him do that again.

Dom frowned and looked away. The wind picked up, and her familiar Chanel scent washed over him. Lust coiled and tightened in his gut. His dick sparked to life. He closed his eyes against the ache in his groin, but the move only amplified the pain behind his eyes. Cursing, he pushed his fingers beneath his sunglasses and pressed them against his closed lids.

"Dominic?" Her voice was filled with worry and concern. "How bad is it?"

"You can't imagine," he replied without thinking and before he realized she was referring to the head on his shoulders and not the one below his belt.

Even with his eyes closed, he knew when she moved, stood and came closer. She brushed her fingers over his temple, smoothed his hair back.

He groaned aloud.

"It will get better," she said softly.

"No, it won't."

64

"It only feels like that now." She stepped between his knees and removed his sunglasses.

He kept his eyes closed or she would see what track his thoughts ran along. "Rebecca."

"Let me look at you." She cupped his face in her hands—both hands, meaning she'd tossed the cone. "Open your eyes, Dominic."

Fuck. Taking a deep breath, he did as she asked.

She sucked in a breath as she stared into his eyes. Yeah, he could just imagine what she saw there. But she didn't move, she didn't do the smart thing and run. Not even when he settled his hands on her hips and said, "I forgot that you eat ice cream with the same enthusiasm as you fuck."

Her mouth dropped open. One copper eyebrow rose. "I forgot how blunt you can be."

He'd never been very good at editing anything before it came out of his mouth. She continued to stare at him, then something in her gaze changed. His fingers flexed, dug into her flesh, the denial of her was too hard to fight any longer. "Rebecca."

His blood throbbed through his veins. He slid his hands up the sides of her body, stopping below her breasts. Her nipples hardened and peaked through her thin sweater, and he shuddered. Her pupils dilated, her lashes drooped heavily as she drew in a deep breath. Shifting his hand, he rubbed his thumb back

65

and forth along the bottom of her breast. Her breathing hitched audibly, so he did it again. He slid his hand higher, until the hard pebble pressed against the center of his palm.

She closed her fingers around his wrist, and whispered, "No." But her gaze was locked on his mouth. As her tongue shot out and licked her lips, a sound very close to a growl rumbled in his throat. He eased her closer. "No," she repeated, just as softly as the first time.

A tremor ran through him. He flexed his hands as he fought the need to taste her, to pull her between his thighs and have her open for him. With a deep breath, he released her.

She took a step in retreat, but remained too close for his comfort.

He drew another deep breath, fought the urge to reach down and adjust his straining erection. "You're going to want to move a little farther away than that." He figured his intent was written all over his face. She swallowed and stepped back again.

"Farther."

"Dom…" Her words trailed off as he gave in, reached down, and adjusted himself.

She stared at the blatantly obvious bulge behind his zipper. "Maybe you should take me home now."

Dominic pushed his hands through his hair, welcoming the jab of pain as the move pulled at his injury. He placed his elbows on his knees, tipped his face toward the ground and closed his eyes. "Give me a minute. I'm not ready to be locked in a car with you yet."

CHAPTER FIVE

Sirens sliced through the early evening air, echoing off the side of the hospital and nearly deafening Rebecca as she stepped out into the ambulance bay. Normally, she waited for patients to be brought in by the EMS crew, but she was restless and had been all shift. Haunted by a desire to do more, even as she struggled against a nagging sensation emergency medicine was not where she belonged.

Coming to that realization while facing a pediatric trauma was not a good omen, yet here she was, in step with the *beep-beep-beep* as the rig backed up. With a deep breath to center herself, she pulled open the rear door as soon as it stopped. "What have we got?"

"Three-year-old male run over in his driveway. Father reports the child was in the back seat unrestrained when he opened the door and fell out while the vehicle was reversing."

As the medic continued feeding her pertinent information, Rebecca focused on her patient. Despite manually being fed oxygen through an endotracheal tube, his skin was pale and clammy, which made the widespread petechial hemorrhage over his upper chest impossible to miss. His abdomen was distended and marked by patterned bruising. Her stomach twisted painfully as she identified the pattern as that of a tire.

"Patient was unresponsive and in mild respiratory distress at the scene, then stopped breathing five minutes out. Heart rate has held steady at 150, BP is—"

"Blood pressure is dropping," the second medic interrupted. "We're losing him."

No way. Not on my watch.

They burst through the doors at a jog, jockeying around a startled young woman standing frozen in the center of the hallway. A few more steps and they arrived in the trauma bay, where they moved the child onto the ER's gurney and quickly attached him to the heart monitor and crash cart.

"Get me c-spine, chest, abdomen, a trauma panel, and blood gas," Rebecca ordered as she began her head to toe examination, gliding her hands over the child's body. "Where is the father now? The mother?"

Karmen stepped in and wrapped a trauma I.D. band around the tiny wrist.

"Father hitched a ride with the uniforms on the scene. No mention of the mother," one of the medics replied.

Rebecca's vision tunneled on the patient as she performed a primary survey—ABCDE:

airway, breathing, circulation, disability and exposure. Her main concern was internal bleeding. And although the medic continued to manually supply oxygen via the ambu bag, she wasn't happy with the rise and fall of the boy's chest. A quick check with her stethoscope showed absent breath sounds on the left side.

"Get me a chest tube." She poured betadine over the boy's chest as a tray was placed within reach. "Who's on for surgery tonight?"

"Dr. Connelly," Karmen answered. "I haven't seen him yet."

"Get him down here." Rebecca inserted the catheter and stepped aside as bloody fluid flowed out the tube. "He's got a hemothorax. I need O neg uncrossed blood."

A nurse handed her the connective tubing for attachment to the drainage system. It worked by replacing the negative pressure in the chest, which in turn reinflated the lung. What she'd wanted to happen – the patient's breathing would ease and blood pressure would improve – didn't.

An alarm sounded.

Someone swore.

The boy's blood pressure continued to fall.

"Start a second line and get that O neg hung," Rebecca ordered.

He was just a little boy. Small for his age. Hair the color of milk chocolate. Knees scuffed in a way that told her he enjoyed roughhousing—as a lot of boys his age might.

A cold sweat trickled down her back as she checked heart sounds. The bleeding in his chest was causing blood to pool around his heart and impede its function. Without surgery, he wasn't going to make it.

"Heart rate's bradying down," the nurse called out.

Damn it! No way was she giving up without a fight. "Karmen, get a cardiac surgeon down here!"

Splashes of betadine and blood turned her gloves brown and red. Rebecca snapped them off, revealing a fresh pair beneath. "Atropine, point zero two milligram. Push that blood." She placed the heel of her hand in position, glanced at the medic still manually feeding the child oxygen and began chest compressions. One hundred compressions a minute without stop.

Focusing on her task, the rest of the world slipped away. There was nothing but her, the tiny body beneath her hands, and the monitors that – no matter how hard she wished otherwise – didn't change. She heard a voice come to here as if from a great distance asking if she needed help. Still she concentrated on those monitors.

Hoping.

Praying with every compression that she could bring him back.

His skin was cool beneath her hands. Each press, meant to deliver oxygenated blood to his brain, only amplified the boy's dire state. His chest, unstable from the crush injury, gave more than normal. His ribs cracked.

Bile rushed up the back of her throat.

Rebecca didn't stop. If she could just bring him back, he could pull through. Children were resilient – more so than adults. Sweat began to trickle down her back, her temples. Her hands cramped.

She halted her compressions. "Check his pulse."

"Dr. Dahlman." That distant voice spoke. Closer this time. Gentle and familiar.

The nurse shook her head. "No pulse."

Rebecca wasn't ready to give up. Not yet. "Epi, push another unit of blood."

"Dr. Dahlman."

All activity around the patient's bed came to a halt.

"What are you all standing around for?" They stared at her like she'd grown a third head. "I gave you an order."

"Rebecca," Nathan said softly. "Call it."

When had he arrived? How much time had passed while she was lost to everything except the young life beneath her hands?

The life she'd failed to save.

Her shoulders drooped and she blew out a breath. "Time of death six fifty-four p.m."

****

Rebecca leaned against the cool tile wall, swallowing back emotion, desperately trying to compartmentalize what she was feeling and get herself under control. Her knees trembled and not just from the crash as adrenaline left her body. Her breath caught. Her gut twisted. Forcing herself to ignore it, she pushed off the wall.

Only to be stopped short when Karmen stepped in front of her. "Are you all right?"

"Sure, why wouldn't I be?" she asked in a shaky voice.

Karmen had brownish black hair that hung in curls just past her shoulder blades, perfect bow lips Rebecca would have sacrificed a few IQ points for, and large expressive brown eyes. She also had a blunt, in-your-face honesty to be admired. "I don't know, maybe because you're ghostly pale and trembling like a newly graduated medical student on the first day of their internship." She stared at Rebecca for a long moment. "You've never taken control like that and done chest compressions. It's unconventional."

She was right. As a doctor, Rebecca normally stepped to the end of the gurney where she could observe everything and shout out orders. Yet today, that hands' off approach hadn't felt like enough.

"Bec? Talk to me, sweetie."

"I'm fine," she replied in a tone designed to

stop any argument to the contrary. "I have to go speak with the boy's fath—"

"Owen."

"What?"

"His name was Owen. Owen Masters. I could go with you. To speak with the father."

"Now who's being unconventional? No, I can handle it. "

Karmen nodded, her brown eyes filled with relief and sympathy.

Rebecca wiped her palms on her scrub pants, then started down the hall, heading for the family waiting room and the toughest part of her job. She stepped into the room, thankful to discover it was empty except for a bald-headed man sitting in a chair and a uniform officer leaning against the wall ten feet to his right. The seated man had his head down, elbows atop his thighs, hands hanging between his knees. His wrists were secured with handcuffs.

She didn't ask what the man had done to earn his police escort. The only thing that mattered at the moment was informing him of the loss of his son. "Mr. Masters?"

His head rose. His eyebrows knitted in a frown, he pinned her in place with his hawkish gaze. "Yes. Who are you? Where's Owen? I want to see Owen."

"I'm so sorry, Mr. Masters."

He blinked rapidly as if warding off her words. His face turned ashen.

Rebecca stepped closer in an instinctive act of comfort. "We did everything we could, but your son's injuries were too severe. I'm sor—"

Her words were cut short as he launched out of the chair with a strangled cry, plowing into her and taking her with him to the floor. His weight slammed atop her, driving the air from her lungs. Hands circled her neck, tightening as his screams filled the air. "You bitch!"

Footsteps sounded from across the room. The uniformed officer appeared behind Masters, who continued to yell.

"You killed him! You killed my son!"

She clawed at his hands, trying without success to loosen his grip as panic set in. Her heart beat a frantic rhythm in her chest. The officer grabbed him beneath the arms and tugged. Relief flared as she was able to take a deep breath. Until the back of her head glanced off the floor.

The uniformed officer managed to get Masters to release his hold around her neck but struggled to remove his weight from her body. Masters leaned down, the smell of whiskey on his breath overpowering. "You'll pay for this bitch. You'll pay for killing my son."

A second uniform appeared. Together with the first, they wrestled a still screaming Masters to the floor. "Owen! I want to see Owen! I want to see my son!"

"Rebecca?"

She startled before the identity of the voice registered, shrinking away from the hand on her shoulder. Embarrassment flared, followed immediately by a coughing spell as she gulped air too quickly.

"Sweetie?"

Karmen. It was Karmen kneeling by her side, worry evident in the slight tremble of her hands as she replaced one atop Rebecca's shoulder, and curled the other around her elbow for support. "Can you stand?"

"Of course I can," Rebecca replied. Getting her feet to cooperate was another matter. She was thankful for Karmen's steadying hand as the uniforms hauled Masters out the door.

"What the hell happened?" Karmen asked.

"Mr. Masters feels I'm to blame for the death of his son."

"That's ridiculous. You did everything possible to save that boy." It wasn't until Karmen pushed her hand out of the way that Rebecca realized she was cradling the back of her head. "Here, let me see." She parted the hair to get a better look. "Did you smack it on the way down?"

"No. It's nothing, just a bit sore."

"It's nothing," Karmen agreed after a brief inspection. "Your throat on the other hand..."

"My throat is fine, too." Rebecca replied, ignoring the stares from the crowd that had gathered.

"It's already bruising."

Brushing her fingers across the neck, Rebecca frowned. "That's not at all surprising with my coloring." Turning on her heel, she made her way back toward the nurse's station.

Karmen jogged a few steps to catch up. "Rebecca, please."

She kept walking, unsure how to explain to her friend that any discomfort she was feeling was nothing compared to the agony Mr. Masters felt. Or that were she to stop long enough for an exam, long enough to allow the happenings of the last hour to take hold, she just might succumb to the anger and fear that warred inside her.

CHAPTER SIX

By the time Rebecca returned home after her shift it was nearly one in the morning. She dragged the band out of her hair, allowing the length to fall down around her shoulders, and headed for a warm shower sure to remove the kinks from her neck. She kicked off her shoes and pulled her shirt over her head as she went. The sharp trill of her doorbell stopped her.

Who in the world is outside my door at this time of night? After the evening she'd had, company was the last thing she wanted. After returning to the door, she peeked through the viewfinder. "What do you want, Nathan?" she asked, holding her shirt in front of her breasts even though he couldn't see her through the closed door.

"I thought you might need someone to talk to."

She sighed. Why did everyone think she was going to fall apart? First Karmen, now Nathan. "I'm fine. I've been through worse."

"Have you?" he asked, his voice pitched lower than normal.

"I've lost patients before." Every physician

78

had.

"But you've never been physically attacked afterward."

Rebecca swallowed hard, as memory of her earlier panic flared with his matter of fact statement. Thankfully, Karmen had been wrong and all evidence had faded with the exception of one lone mark. She fingered the bruise, then pulled her shirt on and the door open.

Nathan's gaze dipped to her neck. His eyes darkened, a frown forming on his forehead.

"I'm tired Nathan, it's been a long day."

"You should really have allowed someone to check you out. The bruising is minimal but the potential for complications is another story. Strangulation can cause—"

Rebecca held a hand up, palm out, stopping his clinical description of possible side effects. The last thing she needed right now was a reminder of how much worse the situation could have been. "I know all about the possibility of complications," she reminded him. She'd been lucky to have come away from it with only minimal swelling and a sore throat.

"Then you know how important it is to—"

"Nathan, please. Is that why you dropped in? To lecture me? Because honestly, I'm too tired. I have no interest in talking through the day's events or hashing out what I'm feeling or thinking."

"No, of course not. I...wanted to see you. I

was worried about you."

A multi-car MVA had come in immediately following the code on the young boy. Nathan had been in surgery for the remainder of Rebecca's shift.

"I was worried about you," he repeated, shifting closer, right up into her space. Without warning, he pulled her into his embrace and touched his mouth to hers.

Rebecca went very still. Placing both hands on his chest, she took a step back, forcing Nathan to release her.

He slid her a long, questioning look. "I don't suppose this has anything to do with the return of your musician?" He didn't wait for a response. "Of course it does." Turning on his heel, he stepped out the open door before turning back. "He won't stay this time either, Rebecca. Men like him are never in it for the long haul."

"Men like him?"

"Arrogant, too-handsome-for-their-own-good."

A grin broke free. Didn't he see he was describing himself?

"He's a rock star for Christ sake."

The grin faded. "You should go."

"You deserve better, Rebecca."

"Thank you, Nathan, but when I require your opinion on something I'll ask for it." And with that, she closed the door in his face.

Damned arrogant, too-handsome-for-his-

own-good stuffed shirt! She hadn't asked for his opinion, she didn't want his opinion and frankly what the hell did his opinion matter?

It didn't. It absolutely did not.

Except, she feared the same thing—that no matter the reason behind Dominic Price's return, he wasn't in it for the long haul. No matter how much she wished otherwise.

Damn it.

With a sigh she leaned against the door and closed her eyes. What had been the point of Nathan's visit? He'd claimed he was worried about her then what does he offer? Clinical rhetoric followed by a passionless kiss? Oh, how she wished she could hit rewind and start this day over.

A knock sounded directly opposite her head. Rebecca startled. "Go away, Nathan," she said without opening the door.

"Who's Nathan?"

Dom. The surge of excitement coursing through her cemented the fact that she was in trouble. Big trouble. She opened the door with a smile on her face. "It must be my night for visitors."

"It's a beautiful one. I wanted some air. Thought I would see what you were up to."

"You have a habit of doing that." Not that she minded all that much.

He shrugged, a move that pulled his black tee even tighter across his shoulders and afforded her a glimpse of abs she knew were flat and ridged. The dark sunglasses were nowhere to be seen. "You're not going to tell me to sod off, as you obviously did with this Nathan bloke, are you?"

She glanced at her driveway, where the motion light on her garage illuminated a sleek black convertible, top down. "Rolling down the windows just isn't the same, huh?"

"Not really, no."

"So, it didn't have anything to do with feeling emasculated driving a minivan?" He cursed beneath his breath. Her smile grew. "What is that thing? Is that Noah's infamous convertible?" The one Dom had mentioned after his accident.

"First, it's not a thing, it's an Aston Martin. And yes, it's Noah's." By his tone, Rebecca guessed she was supposed to be impressed by the brand. His eyebrows slashed downward. "Tell me you know what an Aston Martin is."

"Horribly overpriced?"

"Worth every pound. She's performance and elegance in one damn fine automobile. Look at her lines. She's got style and grace combined with raw horse power."

He was pretty passionate about the car wasn't he? "Do you two need a moment alone?"

"Ha-ha."

She laughed, which had the unfortunate side effect of a brief coughing spell. Dominic's gaze turned cold as steel.

He stepped across the threshold. Close enough she could feel the soft caress of his breath on her cheek. He lifted a hand and gently brushed his knuckles along her neck. "What happened?"

"An incident at work. It's..." her explanation trailed off as he cradled her face in his hand. He brushed his thumb over her cheek, her chin, then finally her bruise as he lowered his hand to her neck. His touch was feather light. Still, she couldn't stop the tremble that worked down her legs or the tears that burned her eyes.

"Becca?"

It was the genuine concern in his voice that pushed her over the edge. Unable to say anything, she shook her head and stepped into his body. He wrapped his arm around her back. The other shifted to cradle her head. Rebecca pressed her face against his chest as tears wet her cheeks.

"I've got you," he said softly.

Fear and sadness coalesced, settled like a lead weight in her chest making a deep breath difficult. Her breathing hitched as she struggled for control. If she lost it now, she may never get it back.

"It's okay, I'm here for you."

His words, murmured against her hair, were intoxicating. She drew his clean, masculine scent into her lungs while his heart beat steady beneath her ear. Her pulse slowed to match his. Her tears ebbed then stopped. Easing back, she looked up into the vibrant blue of his eyes and found something there she couldn't name.

Something she was too afraid to hope for.

"Dominic," she whispered, sliding her hands up his chest and into his hair. She pressed closer, lifted her chin and brought her mouth to the whisper of space right beneath his.

The door closed with a snap. Spinning her around, he pressed her against it, one hand on either side of her head. Against her lower belly, he was deliciously hard and thick. Heat pooled in her loins. Her stomach clenched, her breasts tightened. She pressed her lips to his once, twice. On the third kiss she tugged at his lower lip with her teeth.

He growled low in his throat, tilted her head back and devoured her. He kissed her like she belonged to him. As if the years they'd been apart never existed. He fisted his hand in her hair, slid the other down her body to cup her breast, rasping his thumb back and forth over her nipple, making it stand at attention. She couldn't hold back her moan.

His kiss was as powerful as ever, more so, for she knew where it could lead. He played her body better than anyone before or after him, knowing just where to touch and for how long. The depth of penetration to send her over the edge again and again.

Right before he slipped out the door and disappeared.

Again.

For the second time that night, Rebecca pushed free of a man's embrace.

Shifting away, she walked a few steps before turning back and finding his gaze on hers, silent and assessing. She dropped hers to the bulge filling out the front of his jeans and her throat tightened. She ached with the need to touch him, open her body to him.

Only self-preservation kept her still.

"I can't do this again, Dominic. Do you have any idea what you did to me? How low I sank, crying all over Noah, begging him to tell me where you'd gone, how I could find you?"

His body tightened, making it very clear this was the first he'd heard any of it. "Noah?"

"He didn't tell you about that? I went looking for you at Noah's." He'd lived in Sacramento then, not far from her condo. "The minute he opened the door I knew you were never coming back. It was written all over his face."

"Rebecca—"

"Go away, Dom."

He hadn't taken his gaze off her, and his eyes were filled with frustration, hunger, and bewilderment. "I did come back."

She shook her head. "Why now? For nearly three years you've been content *not* to be with me."

"The hell I was."

"You never—"

"I called you. You shut me out."

"You called me? You *called* me?" Rebecca had to purposely draw in a breath and let it out again. She was trembling, her body vibrating. "Four months, Dominic. You called me four months *after* you walked out."

"I never meant to hurt you," he said, his voice gentling.

"Never meant to hurt me? You made love to me, led me to believe I was important to you and then you walked away without a word." The backs of her eyes stung with disappointment and grief. "Damn you. I told you I loved you. Do you remember what you said to me?"

"I remember," he whispered.

"*Fuck.*" He flinched. "I told you I loved you and you said *fuck.*"

"Becca, please." He scrubbed a hand over his face as she continued, tossing his words back in his face.

"No, I believe it was, *'Why do women always have to do that?'*" Just saying the words again brought back the agony she'd experienced at first hearing them. Her stomach soured. Her breath hitched. "You felt the need to point out how many times you'd heard the words, but I'd never said them before. Do you have any idea how difficult it was for me to tell you?"

Dominic heaved a breath and his shoulders

fell. "I know. I know that now. I'm sorry."

"I'd waited nearly all my life to tell someone I love them and what did you do? You walked out. No goodbye. Fuck off. Nothing." She shook her head, wanting so badly to understand. "Was it that horrible? The thought of loving...of me loving you that you ran all the way back to London?"

"Damn it," he stalked away, pivoted and stalked back. "I was scared, okay? Afraid to admit you mattered to me. Afraid that you might not..." His voice was tight, desperate as he continued. "I was afraid and I ran. A mistake, yes, but one I've had to live with ever since. I can't even look at another woman without comparing her to you. I haven't had sex with anyone but my own fist in three years."

She startled for a minute, but only a minute. How was she to believe him after the ease with which he'd walked away? "Bullshit."

"It's true. The only sexual gratification I've had is tossing off in the shower."

Once upon a time the sun rose and set with him. No more. She didn't think she'd survive another heartbreak at the hands of Dominic Price. "Is that supposed to make me all tingly inside? Make me forget how much you hurt me? I haven't had that problem."

"You haven't..." Dom leaned against the door, dropping his head back and closing his eyes. "Of course you haven't."

87

"You never called after that first time. You never came to see me, even though I know you've been back to the States since then, back in California. It took you being wheeled into my hospital, strapped to a backboard, for me to see you again."

"You shut me out."

"One phone call." Tears squeezed her throat until it was hard to breathe. "You didn't even try."

"Becca," he whispered, pushing off the door and stepping in her direction.

"Don't," she warned.

"I wish I'd handled things differently. I'm sorry, love."

"Spare me your meaningless platitudes. They may have worked on me once, but I've..." Her sigh sounded defeated even to her own ears. "We were just sex, Dom. I understand that now."

He met her gaze, his blue eyes fierce. "We were more."

"No. You didn't even know me."

"I know you, Becca," Dominic said in a low voice that brushed across her senses like a caress. "I know every curve and dip of your flesh. I know how to touch you to make you come for me. To make you scream."

"I don't scream."

"You do for me."

An involuntary shudder worked through her.

"Incredible sex, yes, but still just sex. I want more than that now; a lover *and* a friend."

"We were more."

"No we weren't. What kind of music do I listen to?"

"Classical."

"Anything else?"

"I don't know."

"What kind of car did I drive?"

"A Ford."

"Three years ago?"

"I..." He scrubbed a hand over his face, clearly frustrated. "What does is matter what kind of car you drove?"

"That very first night you took me in the back seat of that car." God, she'd been out of her mind for him, totally out of control. Only he had ever been able to make her lose control. "And you don't remember." She didn't wait for him to respond. "What's my best friend's name? Have you ever met my best friend? Do you remember?"

His confusion was obvious. "I—"

"You never wanted to. It wasn't important to you. What makes me laugh?"

"I do."

"What makes me cry?"

For a moment, she didn't think he was going to answer. Then he did, his voice full of regret. "I do."

He did. He made her cry. White-hot pain

filled her chest. Without her permission, a tear broke free. She brushed it away with an angry swipe. "Go away, Dominic. Leave me in peace."

"Don't give up on me, Rebecca. I've changed."

"Really?"

"Yes." The force of his reply took her by surprise.

"So you're ready for a commitment? Ready to be with me and only me?"

"You think I would cheat on you? Jesus, that's flattering."

"You believe you're ready?" she restated.

"Yes."

"For how long? Forever?"

He didn't even hesitate. "Yes."

Oh, God. Her heart actually skipped a beat. "How am I to believe that? You're still a damn gypsy. You live out of a suitcase, move from friend's spare bedroom to friend's spare bedroom. Do you even have a home?"

"I have a flat in London."

"How much are you there?"

"I'm a musician. I spend a whole lot of time on the road."

His reluctance to answer her question made her push harder. "And when you're not on the road...How much time do you spend in one place?"

"Bec."

"At your flat in London, how much time, Dom?"

"Not much," he admitted.

"Are you happy living like this?"

He was quiet, studying her a minute. "I used to be. Now I want more."

Rebecca could only stare at him, her heart warring with her head. The first wanted her to cross to him and pick up where they'd left off. The latter warned her it would only lead to heartbreak. "You'll be here at least another year, but a car, a place of your own, these are too much of a commitment for you. How can I believe you truly want to commit to me?"

"I never stopped thinking about you, not even for one day."

She shook her head.

He closed the distance between them, cupped her face in one hand and made her look at him. "Yes. Regret will do that to a person."

She didn't step aside and break the connection like she knew she should. She needed this last touch before pushing him away for good. It had taken her all the time they'd been apart not to dream about him every night. Not to wonder where he was or what he was doing. Whether or not he was happy without her.

"The night of my accident, when I opened my eyes and you were there? Seeing you again, Rebecca..." Dominic swallowed hard. "It was like someone let the air back into the room."

God, he was beautiful. It wasn't fair just how

beautiful. But she couldn't do it again, couldn't survive another loss like the last time he walked. "You had your chance. You didn't want me."

"Don't do this. I still believe in us."

She laughed without humor, forcing back the tears trying to break free. "Us? There is no us. You threw us away like yesterday's trash."

"Don't give up on me," he pleaded, his voice hoarse.

Emotion clogging her throat, she forced herself to say the words. "You're too late. I don't love you anymore, Dominic."

Dominic jerked like she'd hurt him. He dropped his hand and retreated a full step. The pain in his eyes was enough to cause the tears she'd been holding back to break free. Her breath stuttered out. She had to fight the urge to curl her fingers in his shirt as he stepped back again, his expression hollow.

His gaze never left her face as he backed to the door, where he finally turned away from her. God it hurt. It hurt so damn bad she couldn't breathe.

He curled his hand around the knob and pulled the door open. Centered in the doorway, he froze as she said softly, "Please don't stop by again."

He tipped his head once in understanding, then he was gone.

Rebecca's stomach heaved. Her knees gave

out and she sank to the floor, no longer able to hold back the sobs that wracked her body.

****

This time he was smarter. Dominic didn't race down the road trying to outrun the memories. He pulled over and let them come.

"Don't," he warned.

"Don't what?"

He crawled out of bed, pulled his jeans on and looked down at her. "Ruin everything by bringing love into this."

Rebecca sat up, the sheet falling away from her freckled breasts, reddened from the attention he'd just bestowed upon them. Christ, she had an incredible body. He could spend hours lost in her. Just had actually. The desire to return to her was overwhelming. Until she uttered those words a second time.

"I love you, get over it."

"Fuck!"

There was no mistaking the flash of pain in her eyes. "Gee, just what every woman wants to hear after she confesses her feelings to a man."

"Do you know how many times someone's said that to me?" He shoved his arms in his shirtsleeves, his feet into his shoes. "'Oh, Dom, I love you, Dom.' They never mean it."

"Yeah? Well consider yourself lucky." Her voice was tight, filled with sadness. "No one's

ever told me they love me."

That gave him pause. "Bec—"

"I'm not some groupie, Dominic. I'm a grown woman. I know my own feelings."

He sighed. "Do we have to do this?"

She shoved the sheet aside and scooted to the end of the bed. "Yes," she said, snagging his hand. "We have to do this."

He stared at her, then at their joined hands for a long moment. "What do you want from me, Becca?"

"Nothing."

"No?" he scoffed. Every woman wanted something. No one uttered those words without an ulterior motive.

"I want you to know what's in my heart. I love you, Dominic."

He felt the truth of that in his bones. He shook his head as panic welled within him. Not knowing what to do with it, he turned and walked out the door.

Dom couldn't breathe. No matter how he struggled, there was no way to draw enough oxygen into his lungs. He was drowning – without a speck of water in site. He gasped and promptly choked. The pain was all encompassing, like nothing he'd experienced before. His limbs felt heavy, weighted down, and useless.

He hadn't lied to Rebecca. He'd heard those

four words so many times. He'd lost count how many. Shouted at him after a show, or whispered during sex, they were just words. Words that meant nothing...until she'd uttered them.

If only he hadn't walked away. Panicked at the realization a woman could affect him both physically and emotionally. But the feelings she'd stirred in him had been so new and terrifying that he'd run.

All the way back to London.

Only to discover that just because she wasn't with him physically didn't mean he'd been able to let go. The memory of her stayed with him—sunk its teeth into him so deeply that to this day he couldn't look at another woman without thinking of her.

Rebecca.

He had no one to blame but himself. He'd fucked up. For nearly three years he'd lived with that knowledge. He'd gotten used to the ache that was with him every day. The pain that had only grown since being back in the States, living out of Noah and Isabeau's guest room, surrounded by their happiness, an easy love he couldn't imagine but spent his life secretly craving.

"I don't love you anymore, Dominic."

He'd destroyed everything. Brought about the very thing he'd been trying to protect himself against. He'd lost the only woman he'd ever loved.

A crushing weight settled in his chest. He'd always feared being alone and that's just what he was. With no one to blame but himself. He'd arrogantly thought that he could win Becca back with charm and charisma. Now he knew those tricks wouldn't work and he had no recourse. He had nothing. Just the emptiness inside of him, the cold ache of loneliness that swallowed him whole.

CHAPTER SEVEN

The house was pitch black, which fit his mood. It was empty – another plus. Dominic sprawled in one of the four chairs surrounding a low table at the far side of the living room. A bottle of ale in his hand, he stared at the flames licking the glass-fronted fireplace. Just how much would he have to drink to forget tonight? How drunk would he have to be before the memory of the pain, the anguish he'd witnessed in Rebecca's eyes was erased? Becca, tough, confident, can-handle-anything-that-came-through-the-doors-of-the-emergency-department Becca. Near to breaking. Because of him.

Knowing how deeply he'd hurt her was one thing. Seeing it was a whole different story.

Dominic took a long pull from the ale. Then another. He welcomed the burn at the back of his throat. Prayed for numbness he feared would never come.

The beep of the alarm system told him he was no longer alone. More tones as a code was entered into the keypad, then Isabeau's voice carried to him across the polished cherry floors.

"I had a happy childhood. It was…anything

but normal, but I was happy. Before the accident."

"Isabeau," Noah replied softly.

"I spent five years in Hell. Five years, Noah, that's all."

"Five years is a long time."

"No," she said adamantly. "Not compared to what other kids live through. I got lucky. I had Thomas to go back to. I found you. I look at this place, this house...it's..."

"You don't like our home?"

"Of course I do. What I'm trying to say is most people look at me and see a dream life. But I also have demons. You know that better than anyone. Demons after only five years, not a lifetime like some."

Dom's body went rigid as the truth of what she left unsaid soaked into his ale soaked brain.

"That girl tonight, she's being abused. She favored her right side. Someone beat her, probably broke her ribs, and no one cared." The tears in her voice tore at him. "No one would look at her and all she wanted was someone to *see* her."

"You saw her, Isa."

"I've been her. Hiding bruises beneath long sleeves no matter the weather. Wearing baggy clothes because anything else rubs and is too painful."

Jesus. How had he not known this about her? It explained so much. Dom lifted the ale to his lips, then lowered it without taking a drink. He wasn't sure it would stay down.

Unaware of his presence, Isabeau continued. "Longing for someone to touch you – not hit or kick, but caress. Wondering how no one notices what you're going through, then forced to face the cold hard reality that no one *wants* to see it. No one cares. What kind of world are we bringing...?"

Dom's throat burned with the need to vomit. He stood abruptly, desperate to get out of there. For his peace of mind as well as her privacy. His emotions were already raw, this new insight into just how bad her childhood had been only amplified his agony.

Isabeau startled.

"I'm sorry." He touched a hand to the remote on the table, activating the recessed lighting in the cathedral ceiling. "Obviously, this conversation was never meant for my ears. I just wanted you to know I was here before..." Before he threw up. "I'll leave."

"It's okay. I'm going to go lie down." She started for the stairs, stopping only long enough to place a hand on Noah's visibly tight bicep before moving up the stairs and into the master bedroom.

Noah remained silent until the door clicked shut behind her, then he began to swear colorfully, without raising his voice.

"Let me guess," Dom said quietly.

"Whitehorse." John Whitehorse, Isabeau's biological father. The man who'd won custody of her after the automobile accident that killed her mother and scarred her hand. A man who'd never wanted his daughter, only her wealth and success.

Noah's hands tightened into fists. "Every time he caught her playing the piano," he growled, then followed his wife upstairs.

It was too much, too damn much. First Becca, then overhearing Isabeau's confession. The pain and anger coalesced inside him making him feel like he'd been sucker punched. He'd never been any good at dealing with emotion. Just another one of his shortcomings. His first instinct was to run. Second, to break something. Instead, he opened another beer.

Dominic turned his gaze away from the windows as Noah came down the stairs thirty minutes later. "Is Isabeau okay?"

"She's sleeping," he said, dropping into the chair Dom had vacated.

He studied his friend. "You want to talk about it?"

"Fuck no."

Unlike Dominic, Noah didn't drop the f-bomb often. When he did, it was a sure sign of his emotional state.

So, even though a large part of him wanted to walk away, to escape the emotion, the overpowering, overabundance of emotion this night was bringing him, Dom left the window and sat in the chair to Noah's right.

Noah cleared his throat. "Isa's spoken with you?"

"About Whitehorse? Never."

"Fuck," he uttered again, launching out of the chair and crossing to the window. "I mean about..." He scrubbed his hands down his face. "She's bored, Dom."

"Not with you." From everything he'd seen in the past seven months of living under their roof, Dom could say that much with certainty.

Noah mumbled something he didn't catch.

"Is this why you were such a bear to live with while she was in Manhattan?" His friend's relaxed, quiet nature combined with his ability to make things happen made Noah a natural leader. He was the decision maker, the peace keeper, the one who dealt with the stress of being in the music industry better than any of them. Until three days before Dom's car accident, when he'd gone from unnaturally quiet to unnaturally quiet and irritable. "You can't possibly think she wasn't going to come back."

Noah scrubbed his hand over the back of his neck, eased out a breath. "Not that she wouldn't come back, just... Isabeau called me every day."

He knew that, usually overheard part of their conversation. The hardest part for him to hear – when Noah would tell her he loved her.

They made it sound so easy, but Dom knew how difficult it really was.

"You couldn't mistake the joy in her voice. She was with friends, with her father. I don't know, Dom, maybe I pushed her too hard, too fast. She gave up everything to be with me, left it all behind. But after the fire, after everything...I was so afraid of losing her."

He'd come damn close to losing her. To a madman who'd wanted her dead. For hours after that fire Noah hadn't known if Isabeau was alive or dead. Dominic couldn't begin to imagine how difficult that must have been.

Pushing his long black hair out of his face, Dom stacked his hands atop his head. "You are a pushy bastard," he said with levity. When Noah only sighed, he continued. "Do you know what I was doing the night of the accident?"

Noah faced him, his expression a mix of confusion and curiosity.

Damn, anyone else and he would never admit it, but Noah was like a brother to him. After all the years, all the stupid shit they'd shared...

Dom focused on him, standing silent, watching. That's how he was. He didn't usually say much, just observed. Always watching those around him, he didn't miss much either. And he didn't normally lie to himself or make something out of nothing the way he'd been doing these past few weeks. "I took Isabeau's

SUV because—"

"You couldn't find the keys to the Aston."

"Yes. But...look, you two are bloody difficult to be around sometimes. The shared looks, the connection... Christ, Noah, how could you ever question whether she's happy with you? It's so damn obvious." This time it was he who launched out of the chair. He hated the bitterness in his voice. Hated even more the constant unrelenting ache in his chest.

Dom began to pace. "I couldn't take it. The wedded bliss. Your damn caveman antics – the way you carried her to bed the minute she returned from New York. I had to get the hell out of here." He stopped pacing, curled his fingers into the back of the chair. "I was hauling ass, thinking about Becca, how I could have had what you have if I hadn't fucked it up. A woman. A life. Here I was back in California, pissed off and lonely as hell."

"Tell me you didn't run that light on purpose."

"You know me better than that."

"I thought I did." He looked skeptical.

"Fuck, Noah, I'm not suicidal."

"Dom—"

Dominic held up a hand to stop Noah from saying anything. "Isabeau's finding her place here. She's making friends, getting settled in. She doesn't regret marrying you; she's just looking for something. Maybe a way to reconcile her past." Jesus, he couldn't imagine carrying around that kind of weight. "Maybe just something to keep her busy while we record. To find her own identity apart from you. I don't know. But I think you do, and I think what's really eating you is that you're worried about her."

Noah stared at the piano. "I don't know how to help her."

"You want to fix everything, that's how you are, that's *who* you are. But you can't fix this for her, Noah. You have to let her find her own way."

"I know that, I do."

Dominic followed Noah's gaze to the gleaming, black, baby grand that had been a centerpiece to the room since Isabeau'd moved to California. "I know you do. I also know how difficult this is for you. Now that I know about Whitehorse, I understand her struggle. She may or may not find her way back to the piano, but at least she has you, and she's composing. She'll work through it with her compositions. She'll put her soul into her music and come out better for it."

"Isa hated performing."

"Really?" For Dom, that was the best part of being a musician.

Noah shoved his hands in his pockets and dropped his gaze to the floor. "Said she felt like a...curiosity." Dom could tell by the look on

Noah's face that wasn't what she had said. "But she loved to play."

Loved. Past tense. "She must want to again, otherwise why torture herself by keeping that thing in the center of the living room, where she has to look at it every day?"

"I don't know how to help her," Noah repeated. "What the hell am I supposed to do when the past sneaks up on her?"

He had no idea, since his own past was giving him a one-two punch right now. "You might not be able to help her."

Noah pulled his hands out of his pockets and shoved them through his hair. "Fuck that!"

"I believe my living here has had a very negative affect on your language, mate."

His lips twisted.

"I don't know what to tell you, Noah. I guess just do what you do best."

"Distract her with sex?"

"Listen," Dom corrected with a grin. "Listening is what you do best."

"Says you." Noah sighed. "I like my idea better. I'm not sure how many more details I can stomach."

"I can't imagine." After returning to his chair, Dominic picked up his ale. "Thank you for never sharing any of it with me." His pain-filled childhood was already a weight around his neck. Learning the details of Isabeau's was a burden he didn't think he could carry.

Noah kicked his feet up on the table, tipped his head to rest on the back of the seat and tossed his arm over his eyes. It was a moment before he spoke, "There's something she's not telling me."

Dom thought back to the past week. The fact he couldn't stand to be in the studio meant he'd spent more time with Isabeau than usual. "You're making something out of nothing."

"Yeah? Why are you so smart about my relationship?"

"Because it isn't *mine*. I'm an idiot when it comes to my own."

Noah laughed softly. His posture relaxed. "About Becca."

"What about Becca?" Dominic asked, tipping the bottle to his lips.

"You're not planning to screw it up again, are you?"

He'd already done irreversible damage to their relationship. Dom cleared his throat, memories forming a thick knot. "Why didn't you tell me she went to you after I left?"

"You were hurting enough already. I figured you'd come to your senses sooner or later."

"And when I didn't?"

"What good would it have done to tell you that when she realized you were gone, she collapsed in my arms and cried? You didn't need that image. You were beating yourself up about it enough already."

He was still beating himself up over it and had to wonder if it would have made a difference to him if he *had* known? Would it have brought him back to her sooner? Or caused him to run faster?

Dom scrubbed his free hand over his face, trading his empty for a fresh bottle when he discovered he hadn't gone numb yet.

Noah watched him pop the top and take a long pull. "How much of that do you plan to drink?"

"Every last bloody one." He tipped the bottle at Noah in a mock salute.

"You want to talk about it?"

"No."

"Because I could always teach you that caveman maneuver," Noah said with a grin. "It worked well for me."

Dom heaved a breath and changed the subject. Throwing Becca over his shoulder and hauling her off to bed wouldn't repair their relationship. Sure, it would be an amazing distraction but when the orgasms were over and reality set back in, she'd probably hate him for it. Giving her another reason wasn't high on his list of wants right now. "How's the record coming along? Alex still referring to *Rapture* as 'slow, emotional vomit'?"

Noah shook his head. "That boy is out of control. You can't rejoin us in the studio fast enough."

He'd be down there tonight, allowing the music to infuse him and push all thought from his mind if he could only tolerate it. "Still feels like the back of my skull is going to come off. Especially when Alex starts pounding out a rhythm on the drums."

"He's so damn young and...energetic."

At twenty-three, Alex was younger than Dominic by seventeen years. "We were the same way at his age."

"Bloody hell, let's hope he matures faster than we did."

Dom chuckled. Maybe he was beginning to numb after all. "He's right, you know. I wouldn't call the song emotional vomit, but cranking it up a notch and boosting the bass would keep it from being too heavy."

"I agree." Noah closed his eyes and sighed. "It's going to go to his head. His ego is already so large I don't know how he fits through doorways."

For some reason that cracked Dom up. Yup, feeling no pain now. When had he become such a lightweight? "Alex has talent, that's why we invited him to join the band. We knew he'd be an asset both onstage and in the studio. Otherwise, any old drummer would suffice."

"Yeah. I'm glad you weren't hurt worse in that accident. Last thing we need is to have to look for another new member."

When Dom narrowed his eyes, Noah smiled.

"That was a long and arduous process. I wouldn't want to have to go through it again."

A shock of pain arrowed through him at the thought of being replaced. Dom shrugged it off. "You know you couldn't go on without me."

"I could. It would be tough but after a week or two—"

"Piss off, you cheeky bastard."

Noah pushed to his feet. "All joking aside, I would appreciate it if you didn't scare me like that again."

"I'll do my best."

He dropped a hand to Dom's shoulder and squeezed. "Thanks. I honestly don't think I could do this without you." Then he headed for the stairs, leaving Dom in stunned silence.

CHAPTER EIGHT

After an endless night of no sleep, Rebecca found herself driving along the foothills of the Sierra Nevada Mountains. She could tell herself the scenery drew her, calmed her frazzled nerves and brought her a bit of peace after a hellish week. And it would be true. Except that peace was not what brought her to Auburn today. Dominic did.

Her mind was still back in her living room, having her say and watching the blood drain from his face and pain fill his eyes. Had been since she'd shed her last tear, picked herself off the floor, and climbed into bed. Where she'd tossed and turned until dawn.

Something had to be done. She only had two days off before another hectic stretch at work. She needed to clear her head and rest up. Which is why, after pacing her house for hours this morning, she'd finally slid behind the wheel of her car.

The sun peeked out from behind the clouds, temporarily blinding her. She adjusted her visor before spotting a woman making her way up the side of the road at a jog. Black ponytail swinging, her pace was steady and sure footed. Right up until she came to an abrupt halt and vomited.

The touchscreen on her dash read 65 degrees outside. Not commonly hot enough to cause heat-related illness, but she didn't want to take the chance. Pulling off to the shoulder, she grabbed her bottled water from the cup holder and got out of the car.

She walked back to where the jogger stood bent at the waist, one hand on her hip, the back of the other pressed against her mouth. "Excuse me."

The woman startled. Her head snapped up, pale grey eyes wide with alarm.

"Isabeau? I didn't mean to sneak up on you. I was driving and saw you stop." Rebecca offered the bottle of water. "Rebecca Dahlman. I met you at the hospital a few nights ago."

"Yes, I remember," Isabeau said, taking the water and rinsing her mouth with the contents.

"Are you okay?" She didn't appear to be out of breath, wasn't sweating heavily, or holding herself in a way that would indicate cramping. "Do you need any help?"

"I haven't been feeling well lately and foolishly thought I could handle a run." Isabeau shrugged and flashed a grin. "I'm fine. A bit embarrassed but otherwise fine."

"Would you like a ride home?"

Her gaze slid over Rebecca's shoulder to

where the car sat idling. She was quiet a moment then nodded. "That would be great. The house is just up the road a bit."

With Isabeau's help Rebecca found the house in less time than it would have taken alone. Everything appeared so different in the daylight, including the home itself. A tall oak was the central feature in the front landscaping, with rock mulch and native plants completing the look. A short rock wall wrapped around the side, disappearing from sight. It was truly beautiful. The type of place Rebecca would love to call home. If not so far from the hospital.

After exiting the vehicle Isabeau stepped to the solid wood front door where she pressed her thumb to a pad. An audible tone sounded, followed by the *click* of the lock disengaging.

It was the first time Rebecca had seen such a set up. "That is slick."

"It still works with a key but makes one unnecessary, which is a plus when you're outside working."

"Or jogging."

"Exactly." Isabeau smiled then pushed the door open. "Come on in."

A black granite entry soon gave way to gleaming cherry hardwood. Leading the way, Rebecca stepped past a hallway that went left, and a sweeping staircase leading to the upper level. Straight through until she found herself centered in the great room, complete with baby grand piano and a panoramic view of the foothills. The giant room was separated into sections with the use of furniture. A couch, two-person lounger, and reclining chair sat atop a rug and beneath a chandelier in the section closest to them. Four chairs surrounded a low table in front of a floor to ceiling fireplace occupied the far end.

"You have a beautiful home, Isabeau."

"Thank you. Noah already owned the house when I met him. He'd picked it up as a foreclosure and had a studio put in the walkout basement but nothing else done. Everything was white at that time, including the kitchen cabinets. I made a few changes."

"Obviously."

The upstairs of the house had been constructed only on the front half of the home, creating a loft effect. Below the loft, next to the entry, was an open kitchen. No longer white, it sported cherry cabinets, granite counters and stainless restaurant-quality appliances.

"Did you come from a large family?" Rebecca asked, a bit stunned by the size of the dining area off the kitchen. Where the longest table she had ever seen in a home sat surrounded by at least twenty chairs.

"I love to cook. On Sundays I make brunch and welcome any friends or family who happen to be in the area. Nick, do you know Nick, the band's guitarist? Nick, his wife Tracey, and

113

their two children usually come. Alex, the new drummer. And Dom, of course."

She blinked in surprise. Dominic? It was hard to picture him in such a domestic scene. "Have you ever filled every seat?"

"Once. King Soul was in town – a band who toured with Black Phoenix years ago." Smile in place, she began ticking off people on her fingers. "They brought their manager, sound and lighting guys, wardrobe mistress, and all three of their bus drivers. I ran out of space at the table."

As an only child who spent most of her youth alone, Rebecca couldn't imagine what it would be like having that many people in her home. Sure, she dreamed of surrounding herself with family – a husband and lots of kids – but what Isabeau described went beyond that. "It sounds hectic."

"It's wonderful. You're welcome to join us anytime. We usually eat around eleven-thirty."

Rebecca nodded and looked around the room, her gaze once again drawn to the piano. "Who plays; you or Noah?"

"I used to. Now I mostly just compose."

"It's an odd coupling, isn't it? A pianist and a rock singer."

Isabeau blinked. She let out a slow grin. "I suppose it is."

"At least there's a connection. You both share a love of music."

"It helped I was a fan of their music before I met Noah at the bar."

"You met Noah in a bar?" It struck Rebecca like the beginning of a bad joke: *A pianist and rock star walk into a bar...* She smiled.

"I know what you're thinking, but you'd be wrong. I owned the bar."

"Do you still have it or did you sell it before you moved?"

"It burned down a week before I came to California. Arson."

Shock rippled through her. "That's terrible. Was anyone injured?"

"Yes," Isabeau replied, her eyes shuttering a bit. "But not the person he was after."

Meaning her. Someone had been after Isabeau, but she'd survived. It was obvious by her closed expression she didn't want to talk about it, so Rebecca changed the subject. She walked away from the piano and closer to the windows with the stunning view. "I had no idea who Dominic was when I met him. I'd never heard of him."

It was the right move, as the shadows immediately left Isabeau's face. "No?" A smile blossomed. "I bet that was a blow to his ego."

There was something about her smile. Rebecca had noticed it at the hospital, too. It lit her up. Took her from okay to beautiful. "He does have quite an ego, doesn't he? By the way, fantastic job with the minivan."

115

"I have no idea what you're talking about," Isabeau said with a straight face. Then a smirk appeared and they both laughed. "He scared the life out of me. Getting that call...I suppose you've noticed he's more than just my husband's closest friend, he's—"

"Your friend, too."

"We're all close, being with each other as much as we are, but Dom and I; he's like the brother I never had."

She nodded and glanced around the room. "Is Dominic here?"

"I was wondering how long it would take before you asked about him." Isabeau was quiet a moment. Her smile turned into a frown. "I believe he's still in bed. Is that normal? The constant headache? He says he's fine, but shouldn't it have stopped by now?"

"A headache after a concussion can linger for weeks." When her reassurance failed to remove the worried look from Isabeau's face, Rebecca added, "I'll take another look at him."

"Thank you. If you go down that hall there, his is the last door on the right."

She turned, started across the room.

"Hold on a sec," Isabeau called. She disappeared into the kitchen, came out a minute later with a mug in her hand. "Take this to him?"

****

Rebecca stood just inside the door and stared. In the quiet, shadowed room, she breathed in a mix of cologne and warm male. Her pulse tripped, her mind blanked.

God Almighty.

Sprawled across the bed, one arm tucked behind his head, Dominic slumbered. He was on his back, naked but for the pale gray sheet riding so low it barely covered one leg and his genitals. She didn't have to wonder what he looked like beneath that sheet. She knew.

Long and thick.

Beautiful.

Without her permission, her eyes took themselves on a tour. Time had been good to him. Damn good. He still had the incredible physique of a man who stayed in shape. He was thin but not scrawny. Olive skin covered hard muscle—a lot of muscle, just not the bulky kind. His chest had just the right amount of hair dusting his pecs. Hair that tapered to a thin line that bisected a flat, ridged stomach and disappeared beneath the sheet.

She inhaled a deep breath then let it out on a quiet sigh. Just looking at him made her desperate to touch him. Her fingers curled inward against the need to follow through on that desire.

The long body stirred and so did something deep inside her. He made a sleepy, gravelly sound as he stretched. His muscles flexed and rippled. Her gaze dropped. Past those lickable abs...

The sheet tented.

Her mouth went dry. Slowly, she lifted her gaze to find him watching her. "I..." She had to clear her throat to speak. "How's your head?"

He brought his hand out from behind his head, down his chest, and slipped it beneath the sheet. He stared at her, bold as could be, as he stroked his impressive length. "It aches."

Dear God. Even knowing he was trying to make her uncomfortable, the sight before her was impossibly arousing. She had to force herself to look away. "I meant the one on your shoulders."

"What do you want, Rebecca?" The question was harsh and hoarsely spoken.

She stepped further into the room. "I want to apologize for last night."

"You changed your mind about going to bed with me?"

She moved her gaze over him, from the hand still cupping his erection, up his arm to his chest, where the white of the wrapping around his ribs stood out against the rumpled sheets. The image of them rolling across those sheets flashed through her mind and she shivered. "I...no. I mean about what was said. I...want to talk to you."

"Yeah? Well, I want to throw you down, climb on top of you and fuck you 'til you scream."

Shock moved through her. Not that he was so blunt, but that her body immediately reacted. She grew wet as her nerves tingled and swelled. Every inch of her prepared to take him as she recalled how it felt to have him on top of her. God, she loved how it felt. The weight of his body. The press of his skin against hers from shoulder to groin. He would brace his forearms on either side of her face, bury his hands in her hair and focus all that intensity on her. Like she was the center of his universe. And at least for that moment, she was.

"You remember, don't you?" She knew that husky murmur, the one he used when whispering in her ear while he drove deep within her body. He always said the nastiest, dirtiest things in that toe-curling accent. No matter how much she'd thought she wouldn't go for that sort of thing, she did. At least from him. "You remember how it was between us."

Her feet propelled her forward one step, then two. "Dom, I—"

"Rebecca," he warned softly. "You take one more step into this room and that's exactly what I'm going to do."

The trembling started in her knees and worked up her body. She didn't doubt he'd do as he said. One more step and there'd be no stopping him. Oh, he wouldn't force himself on her, he wouldn't have to. Once touch and her resolve would crumble. The conversation she needed to have with him, forgotten. Her spine stiffened and she stepped back.

"That's what I thought." The sarcasm did nothing to hide the sadness in his voice.

Dominic threw off the sheet and sat up, completely unconcerned with the fact that he was naked and fully erect. Sitting on the side of the bed, he muttered a few choice curse words as he scrubbed his hands over his face before pushing them through his hair. Then he picked up the jumbo bottle of pain reliever that rested on his night stand, shook a few into his hand, chewed them dry and swallowed before chasing them with the half empty bottle of water.

Rebecca offered him the mug and frowned.

He didn't seem to notice. He closed his eyes and pressed his fingers against the bridge of his nose. His long lashes shadowed his high cheekbones, but did nothing to disguise the dark circles beneath his eyes.

Her frown deepened. If this was how he began every morning – afternoon, she corrected with a glance at the clock – it was no wonder Isabeau was concerned about him. "You should let me examine you."

He met her gaze, a combination of pain and anger apparent in his bright blue eyes. His lips curled in an empty smile. "You did a thorough job of that when you sauntered into my room uninvited. You want a closer look..." He very deliberately let his gaze roam over her. "You'll have to lose the clothes."

She shivered. "I meant your head injury. I know you're pissed off at me right now but...what are you...?"

He stood and moved toward her, slow and easy, like he wasn't in a big hurry. Stalking her, like a wild animal stalked prey. The thought stuck. She was the prey – he, the one about to devour her.

She took a quick, involuntary step in retreat. *Dear Lord.* Her mouth watered and a tight thickness filled her chest. She tried to keep her eyes on his face, but the temptation was too great. She glanced down.

And took another step back.

It wasn't until he lifted a hand to the door frame that Rebecca realized he'd backed her out into the hallway. The smile that curled his mouth told her she'd done exactly as he expected. The sadness that darkened his eyes had her stomach knotting painfully.

She shook her head as he reached out, but it wasn't her he was reaching for. Curling his hand around the mug, he removed it from her slack fingers. Then he closed the door in her face.

The lock clicked.

Dominic turned the lock, then gripped the knob. He closed his eyes, and worked to control an overwhelming urge to go after Rebecca. What had she been doing here, anyway? Hadn't she said enough last night? Was she trying to completely destroy him?

If so, she was doing a damn good job.

He didn't know what hurt more; the pounding ache in his skull or the throbbing in his groin. Waking to her standing over his bed had been like a blow to his solar plexus. He'd become aware of her scent first, then had opened his eyes to find her gaze devouring every inch of him. Damn it, her heart might not want him, but her body did. That had been as obvious as the flush of her cheeks, the way her tongue darted out and wet her lips just before she realized he'd awakened.

But it was also pretty obvious that no matter how much her body wanted it, she wasn't going to give in, so he'd gotten rid of her the quickest way he knew how. It had been just too damn painful looking at her, while her words swam through his memory.

I don't love you anymore, Dominic.

Turning abruptly, Dom crossed the room and entered his private bath. He placed his tea on the vanity, turned on the shower with a flick of the wrist, then stepped beneath the spray without waiting for the water to heat.

His testicles ached. He was hard as a brick.

He wrapped his hand around himself and stroked all the way to the tip and back again.

Emptiness would be all he ever had with Becca, some loser tossing off in the shower.

CHAPTER NINE

"Egads, girlfriend! You look like hell!"

Rebecca burst into tears before the words were even out of her best friend's mouth.

"Oh, shit." One of Karmen's eyebrows arched as she stared at Rebecca, a worried tilt to her mouth. "I'm sorry, sweetie. I didn't mean to make you cry. Come sit on the couch. I'll get you something to drink."

"I'm okay," Rebecca whispered, embarrassment heating her face. "I just need a minute."

Karmen was quiet a moment. "You don't look okay to me," she said, then disappeared into the kitchen.

In spite of everything, Rebecca smiled. Karmen's direct, straight-to-the-point nature was what she loved most about her. In a world full of political correctness and half-truths meant to keep people's feelings intact, honesty, even when it was difficult to hear, was a welcome change.

They'd met when Rebecca was a first-year resident and hit it off right away. Over the course of their friendship, they'd laughed together, cried together, overindulged a few times together, and become each other's rock. Which is why, after being driven from Dominic's bedroom, Karmen's apartment was the obvious destination.

Karmen returned from the kitchen carrying two mugs. She shoved one into Rebecca's hands then sat next to her on the couch. "Talk to me, Bec."

Letting out a long breath, she curled chilled fingers around the mug, greedily soaking up its heat, before lifting it to her lips. But it only served to remind her of the warmth of the cup she'd brought for Dom and how he'd looked naked as the day he was born. "Holy—"Rebecca inhaled sharply, the burn as she swallowed having nothing to do with temperature. "What did you put in this coffee?"

"Bailey's," Karmen replied, then took a healthy swig from her own mug. "You looked like you could use it."

"I'm probably going to pass out on your couch if I drink this. I didn't get any sleep last night."

Mi casa es su casa." Karmen's eyes were warm and full of concern as she sipped her coffee, waiting for Rebecca to start talking.

The problem was, Rebecca didn't know where to begin. She stared down at the mug in her hands. "Nathan swung by my condo last night."

"Yeah? What did he want?"

"Me."

Karmen swallowed wrong and began coughing.

Shifting in her seat, Rebecca patted her back. "Are you okay?"

"Don't worry about me. Explain!"

"He kissed me." If what he gave her could really qualify as a kiss. Which if compared to the second kiss she'd received last night...well, there was no comparison. "One minute he's lecturing me on the possible side effects of strangulation injuries and the next he's kissing me."

Karmen stared at her. "He seriously just planted one on you?"

"He seriously did."

"What a jerk," she said in a disgusted tone. "You've been pretty clear about being done with him, right?"

"I thought I had."

"What possessed him?"

That was the question. Rebecca could only think of one explanation. "It could be that my father has made it abundantly clear Nathan is his choice for me. Which is infuriating. Why does everyone assume that's what I want?"

Karmen shrugged. "I don't assume."

The more she thought about it, the more upset Rebecca got. "If I wanted an arrogant, pain-in-the-ass doctor for a lover, I'd have grabbed onto him with both hands already. I'm

126

thirty-four for God's sake!"

"Ancient. Better be careful, or your eggs will shrivel up and turn to dust."

"They will!"

Karmen sighed. "Talk to me, Bec. What brought you to my door today in tears? It's not Nathan or your father. Is it the little boy from yesterday?"

Her anger dissipated, replaced by a wave of pain and sadness. "No. Not exactly."

Her friend waited, the same emotions mirrored in her eyes.

"Nathan wasn't the only one who stopped by last night."

"Let me guess, Tall, Dark and Studly?"

Rebecca looked away, toward the sliding glass door leading to the balcony. Rays of sunlight slanted through the glass, pooling on the floor. The tiny kitten Karmen had rescued from the side of the highway last month, slept curled in a ball in the patch of light.

"What did he do?" Karmen asked. "Did he kiss you, too?"

She closed her eyes against the memory. "He offered me comfort."

"Between the sheets?"

"Not at first. He just...held me. No questions. Just whispered words of reassurance, his arms around me, heartbeat in my ear."

"Then he ruined it by making a pass," Karmen guessed.

"No. That would be me." Rebecca set her mug on the coffee table and launched out of her seat. She began to pace. "He just smelled so damn good, and felt—"

"Like a hot, sexy rock star?"

"Yes," she said on a whisper. "I don't know what came over me."

She slid Rebecca a long look, a mischievous grin in place. "It's called lust."

Rebecca continued as if Karmen never spoke. "I couldn't stop myself. He smells the same, Karmen, feels...so familiar. I had to see if he tasted the same."

"And?"

"He does. For a minute there, I forgot my name."

Karmen fanned air in front of her face. "Damn."

"Then I remembered. I remembered everything." The sadness, pain and loneliness. Everything she was feeling now.

"Tell me you didn't."

"I pushed him away. I told him to stop coming by, that I didn't love him anymore."

Karmen pulled back, clearly shocked. "Did he believe you?"

"He left." Unable to stand the look on Karmen's face any longer, Rebecca dropped back onto the couch. She pinched the bridge of her nose as a tension headache began to make itself known. "It would be so much simpler if I was attracted to Nathan. He's comfortable. Safe."

"Boring," Karmen sing-songed.

"Dominic is...intense, funny, not comfortable and definitely not safe."

"Don't forget hot as hell and British."

Rebecca frowned. "He's also a bad bet. Future for him means two weeks."

"Sure, it used to. It's been nearly three years."

"People don't change, Karmen."

"People change all the time, Rebecca. Life changes them. The only way for that not to happen is if someone slept through life."

"Don't give up on me, Rebecca. I've changed." Her stomach rolled as Dominic's words popped into her head. "Do you really believe that?"

"We live, we learn. From our mistakes, even our successes. How can that not change a person?"

Rebecca hugged herself, fisting the material of her shirt. "I went to see him this morning," she admitted softly. "I wanted to tell him...."

"What?"

She shook her head. "I'm not sure."

"What happened?"

"I panicked. He was naked and gloriously erect and..." She felt her entire body come alive at the memory.

"And? Don't clam up now!"

"Angry," she whispered. "He's so angry at me. He told me unless I was planning to crawl

129

into the bed with him I could leave."

"Let me see if I'm following you correctly. You had Dominic, buck-ass naked, ready and willing, and you ran away?" Karmen didn't wait for an answer, just continued. "Dominic Price, the man who gets you hotter than Hades?"

"I can't do it again." Let him inside her heart, her body, only to have him leave.

"Do what? Allow a man to worship your body?"

"Karmen," Rebecca sighed.

"I'm sorry. I am, but honey he's a walking fantasy."

"Yes, right before he walks out the door."

"Who says this time he will?"

"I can't go through it again. I only just got over him."

Karmen's response was an unladylike snort. "Ha!"

"What?"

She rolled her eyes. "You haven't gotten over him. You still dream about him. You still remember how he smells, his taste."

"You make me sound like an idiot."

"No. No sweetie, just a woman who was knocked on her ass by a man. You loved him. You still love him, or you wouldn't have gone to him this morning. You wouldn't worry about having hurt him." Karmen studied her for a minute. "I say go for it. Let him take you on the ride of your life. Again."

"And if he breaks my heart? Again?"

"Maybe he won't."

"He will."

"Answer this. You sent him away. What if he stays away?"

"Good." Then she could get on with her life. Stop dreaming about something that would never be.

"Is it?" Karmen asked.

"Of course it is," she said quietly, desperately because it has to be.

Karmen stared at her in disbelief, pinning her in place with her eyes. "Dominic stays away and you never see him again. You just hear about him in the news or through the grape vine. How do you feel about that?" She scooted to the front edge of the couch, her voice dropping. "He gets married—"

"He won't," Rebecca denied. Her heart lodged in her throat at the thought of Dominic with another woman. An ache settled unhappily in her stomach. "He's not the type." But she'd thought he might be. The night in the hospital, she thought he'd married Isabeau. That he'd given his heart to another, when he wouldn't give her the same. Tears burned the back of her eyes.

"Are you going to be okay with this? Will the pain be any less because you didn't give him a second chance to hurt you? Or will you ache even more because you'll always have to wonder 'what if?"

Had she made the right choice? Could pushing him away have been wrong? What if he had changed and he was ready to be with her and only her? Forever. She shook her head, spilling fat tears from the corners of both eyes. "You're not making me feel any better, Karmen."

Karmen flashed a sympathetic smile as she settled a hand atop Rebecca's. "You didn't come here for me to pat you on the back and tell you that you did the right thing."

She hadn't. That's not what Karmen did.

"I'm just saying that if you close this door, it's forever this time. If he has changed, he won't let you hurt him again."

Rebecca sighed, pressed her fingers against her eyelids.

"Do you want my advice?" Karmen asked.

"Yes."

"Fuck him, Bec. Literally. Fuck his brains out."

Her eyes snapped back open. "Karmen!"

"Stop worrying about tomorrow or the next day and live in the moment. Has pushing him away made you feel any better? No? Then pull him closer."

"Could you?"

"Pull Dominic Price closer? In a heartbeat!"

Was she going to live her life in fear of tomorrow? Always pushing Dom away based on what might come to pass? Or could she trust this time would be different? Karmen could pull him closer, maybe she could, too? "Even if you knew he wouldn't hang around for long?"

"Anything is better than going home every night to an empty bed," she said softly. "Life's too short, Rebecca. We see the proof of that every day at the hospital. If there's something you want to say to him, say it. If you want something that so far only he's been able to give you, go get it! Because you never know what tomorrow will bring. Or if you even have a tomorrow."

CHAPTER TEN

Dominic glanced around the room one final time, checking to make certain he hadn't left anything behind. The bathroom was clean, closet empty, and bed stripped. There was nothing left to do but grab his bags and go.

After last night, the choice had been clear. Hell, he'd had no choice. It was time to move on. Move forward. Grabbing his leather duffle in one hand, guitar case in the other, he turned for the door—and froze. Isabeau was playing the piano.

The whirlwind of sound drew him down the hall, until he stood in the entryway, entranced. Whatever the piece she was playing, hers or another composer, it was a soft melody, full of emotion. Her fingers floated gracefully over the keys as she poured her soul into the music.

Without warning she changed tempo and feel. In contrast to the first piece, this one was dark and crude; gut wrenching. It varied in rhythm and dynamics, and could be described as anything but gentle. Pain-filled immediately came to mind. And it was true. He felt it in his chest; cloying, heaving, smothering.

134

Dominic glanced at the closed door leading to the basement, wondering if Noah was still in the studio, if he knew his wife was playing. He would want to know.

Again she changed things up, this time with a totally different genre of music. A grin broke loose as he recognized the song as Black Phoenix's. A song from one of their less popular albums, although she put a different spin on it, and made it her own.

Dominic was torn. Should he go find Noah, or walk in and act like it wasn't a big deal to find her at the piano? He'd seen firsthand the effect playing had on Isabeau while they were in New York. Now that he knew about the abuse...

He sighed. If he hadn't overheard her conversation last night, he wouldn't hesitate. After setting his bags down, he stepped into the room.

At the piano, Isabeau straightened a bit. The music ended abruptly, the sudden silence jarring. She didn't turn to face him, just sat there, her long ebony hair hiding her face as she curled her right hand around her left and settled them in her lap.

"Interesting interpretation," he said, referring to the last song. "That was *Tempted*, wasn't it?"

Isabeau didn't answer.

Dom crossed the room to stand at the side of the piano. "Isabeau?"

She looked up at him, her eyes glassy.

Shit.

What was he supposed to do now? Should he reach out to her, offer comfort? Would she want him to? They'd shared secrets. She told him about her childhood, the loss of her mother. But she hadn't shared this one. What the bloody hell was he supposed to say now that he knew this secret? One she most likely never wanted him to know?

His internal struggle showed, apparently, because she frowned. "The last thing I want is your pity, so wipe that look off your face."

He scrubbed his hand over the back of his neck and did his best to appear unaffected. "Do you want me to get Noah?"

"No!" She gazed at him, seemed to realize her forceful reply hadn't eased his concern and shrugged. "I have to learn to deal with this on my own. I can't always go running to Noah to hold me up."

"Why not? Isn't that what partners do?"

"I'm tired of being the weak little woman."

With everything she'd already lived through in life and survived; she was one of the strongest people he knew. "You're far from weak."

"Noah's probably tired of it, too."

"Are you kidding? Men love that. Makes us feel masculine and strong."

She smiled at him, just a bit, then hovered her right hand over the keys. She played four notes. "So, now you know I have demons."

"I always knew you had demons, luv, I just didn't know what caused them. I can't imagine what it was like for you—"

"Change the subject, Dominic," she said with a vehement shake of her head.

He slid onto the piano bench next to her, ignoring her startled protest as he used his hip to push her over so they both fit. "You know, I've never been a big fan of classical music," he said, repeating the four notes an octave higher. "Becca? She listens to the stuff all the time."

"So, it's growing on you?"

"Hell no!" His heartfelt response pulled a laugh from her. "The piano is nice though and you, you played one of our songs. That's pretty good."

She shot him a dry smile. "You think I'm pretty good?"

She was a bloody musical genius and they both knew it. But Isabeau wouldn't want to hear that, and he sure as hell wasn't about to tell her something people had been saying her whole life. "You're not bad."

She chuckled again and some of the stiffness left her spine. "You're just saying that because you don't want me to notice you're leaving."

Dominic sighed. "You should be happy I'm leaving so that you can have some privacy around here." So she could keep some of her secrets. It wasn't fair to her he'd overheard a conversation never meant for his ears. One she hadn't trusted him with. "I never planned on hanging around this long. I just got...complacent. You and Noah have been married six months now, and you've never spent a day alone together in your own house. It's time for me to get my own place. My own car."

"Careful, you're beginning to sound like you're thinking of putting down roots."

He nudged her with his shoulder. "I've got to grow up sometime. It worked out well for Noah."

She smiled, her eyes warming.

"Isabeau? When you and Noah were dating—"

"Noah and I dated?" she said, turning to face him. "Seriously, we never really dated."

"While we were working on the demo and you two were circling each other like sharks," he corrected, which earned him a laugh. "Did you ever tell him?"

"Tell him what?"

"About your demons." Or was he the only one who kept them secret? Buried in a place deep inside of him where they festered. "Did you share with him why you stopped playing?"

"You know I didn't."

"Why not?"

She pushed her hair away from her face, then propped her elbows on the edge of the piano's keyboard and her chin in her hands. "Fear," she replied as she glanced at him. "Self-preservation, a number of different reasons. If I confessed to him my deepest and darkest secrets and he left...that would be worse than if he left before learning them. It's terrifying, the thought of opening yourself up to someone who has the power to wound you deeply when they leave."

Dominic wanted to ask her what she would have done if he *had* left her. If she would have given him another chance. But Noah never would have walked away. It just wasn't in him. He was the type that set his mind to something, then got it. No matter what it took.

Dom didn't deny that made Noah the better man. "What made you think he was going to leave you?"

"I knew all along he would leave me," she said, her expression serious. "Right up until the moment he proposed."

"Are you for real?" Dominic started to laugh.

Isabeau frowned. "You told me the first time I met you Noah fancied blue-eyed blondes. I'm definitely not a blue-eyed blonde."

He stopped laughing. Dom looked down at her pale eyes, golden skin and ebony hair, and felt a tinge of guilt crawl up his spine. "About that. I was a bit miffed at Noah that night."

"So, it's not true?"

"Oh, it was true enough, but it wasn't something I would ever have told you had I not just gotten off an exhausting flight from London and been facing two months in a hotel only to

139

discover it was all because Noah found a woman who made him hard."

Her eyes widened in surprise. "Dominic!"

"It's true. Jesus, I didn't know what to think. Who the hell does that? Picks a studio on the opposite side of the country from where he lives because of a pretty girl?"

Her eyes were round with shock and full of denial. "That can't be. You're pulling my leg."

"We could have been working in Sacramento," he assured her. "I knew something was up when I got to the hotel in Long Island City and Nick told me where Noah was. Then all I had to do was see how he looked at you and I knew what he had done."

Isabeau just stared at him.

"You can stop grinning like an idiot," Dominic said, even though he was grinning, too. He shook his head. "It's not fear keeping you quiet now, is it? Because, you know, he'll be so chuffed he'll be insufferable."

Isabeau curled her left hand over her flat abdomen. She closed her eyes and sighed.

"Isa, why haven't you told Noah you're pregnant?"

"I've been waiting for the right time," she replied softly.

"How about the moment you found out?"

"I was in New York. I wanted to tell him in person, so I flew back early. Only you were all here, working, and Noah...had other plans for me."

Yeah he had. She'd barely made it through the front door and Noah had her over his shoulder as he carried her up the stairs to their room. "Why not after the 'other plans'?"

"The hospital called."

Shit. He knew he figured into this somehow.

All the more reason for him to leave tonight. Put himself up in a hotel somewhere until he could find a place. Isabeau was fiercely protective of 'her boys' – all four of them. It was an affection they returned. But Dom didn't need her mothering him to the point where her life was put on hold. "I don't know why you haven't kicked me out."

"Why would I?" she asked sincerely. "You're in the studio from noon to midnight, and when not there you're usually in your room."

"Or hanging with Noah." When not recording they spent most of their time talking music, the album, the upcoming tour.

"Who am I to tell you that you can't hang out with Noah? Besides, in case you haven't noticed, I'm rather fond of you," she said, setting her hand atop his.

Dom let out a slow, careful breath and gave her hand a squeeze. "The feeling is mutual. Which is why I'm giving you back your house, your husband, *and* your privacy." He stood and was halfway to door when she stopped him.

"Dominic?" she said softly.

141

He turned, finding her still at the piano, her back to him. "Yeah?"

"How'd you know?"

"You've been mothering me for a week now. All that time together, when I would usually be in the studio, it's hard to miss. You don't drink coffee anymore. You turn green at the oddest moments, over things that never used to bother you. My head might throb like a bitch, but I know the sound of someone retching. It's familiar to me since the accident." A complete understatement. He'd spent the first few days sick as a dog. "Frankly, I think it's obvious. Even with Noah in the studio all day long, I don't know how he hasn't figured it out. He's not one to miss things like this."

"It wasn't supposed to be possible. After the accident...The doctors told me I'd never have kids."

They'd also told her she'd never play the piano again. "Obviously, they underestimated your dedication to the cause."

Isabeau laughed then went quiet. Too quiet. "What if I inherited more than my dark skin and hair from him?" she asked softly. "What if I inherited his temper?"

"I've never seen you lose your temper, not even over some of the stupid shit Alex has done." And he'd done some bloody stupid shit. Most of it in Isabeau's house. "You'll be a fantastic mother."

When she didn't reply, he asked, "Isabeau, don't you want this baby?"

"More than my next breath," she admitted, heartfelt. "It's just surreal, new, and a bit terrifying."

"I get that. But Noah knows something is up. He thinks you're not happy here with him."

"What a pair we are. He's afraid I'm unhappy here, and I'm afraid to tell him I'm—" she stopped suddenly.

Dominic opened his mouth to ask her what was wrong, when Noah spoke, his tone equal parts curiosity and apprehension. "Afraid to tell me you're what?"

She always did have an uncanny ability to know when Noah entered a room, whether or not he was in sight. Isabeau slipped off the piano bench and turned in the direction of his voice.

Dom did as well. He didn't mean to be a part of this conversation, but before he could escape, Noah stepped out of the doorway leading to the basement and into the archway—directly between Dominic and his luggage.

Noah's gaze bounced between his wife and the piano. "Were you playing?"

"The urge has been much stronger these past few weeks."

"That's a good thing, isn't it?" Noah asked, hope in his voice.

"It's...interesting...since it coincides with a

host of other symptoms."

"Symptoms?" His entire body tensed, like a man preparing to take a blow. "Are you ill?"

"I'm not ill," Isabeau reassured him as she crossed to stand before him. She placed a hand in the center of his chest. Noah immediately grasped it, his thumb smoothed back and forth across her palm. "And I'm not unhappy with you," she continued, then reached into her back pocket with her free hand, withdrawing what appeared to be a black and white photograph. She turned Noah's hand and placed the photo into his palm. "I've been exhausted, nauseous, and..."

"Afraid to tell me you're..." She pointed at the photograph and Noah appeared to lose his train of thought. "You're not ill," he said after a moment.

"No. I'm—"

"Pregnant." He answered for her, then looked over at Dominic.

"Why are you looking at me?" Dominic asked, smiling broadly at Noah's stunned expression. "You're the one who can't keep your hands off her."

Noah blinked.

Isabeau beamed up at her husband. "I couldn't believe it either. The ob-gyn had to do an ultrasound to prove it to me, even after I heard the baby's heartbeat."

"You heard..." Staring down at the

ultrasound in his hands, Noah floundered. Choosing not to say much, which was his usual M.O. was one thing. But when he chose to use words, he could usually string a sentence together that made sense. Not so much now. "You're pregnant," he repeated.

"Yes."

Dom wondered how it would feel to learn you were about to have a child. To believe it could never happen, and in the next minute discover that not only could it, but your child was already growing inside your wife.

He couldn't imagine. Never really considered kids a part of his future. The only family he had was Noah and Isabeau. He'd never had a mum, siblings nothing.

But the look on Noah's face...*damn*. Dominic smiled, genuinely happy even as he pondered if he would ever know that kind of joy.

"Isabeau," Noah sighed, his voice pitched so low it was barely audible. He cupped one hand around the back of his wife's neck and the other around her waist, then pulled her into his embrace. He pressed his cheek against her temple. "Isa...you take my breath away."

Okay. Past time for him to leave. Dominic edged toward the door. He picked up his luggage when Noah stopped him.

"Dom?"

He turned back and was forced to drop his duffle and snag the keys out of the air before they smacked him in the face—the keys to Noah's Aston.

"Keep it," Noah said. "Seems I'm going to need one with a bit more space."

CHAPTER ELEVEN

A week later Dominic was finally able to tolerate being in the studio, and happily returned. He'd lost weeks to his concussion. Weeks he needed to make up by putting in more hours a day than the rest of his mates. It wasn't much of a hardship, since he had nothing else to do with his time except sit alone in his apartment.

He hated being alone. When his grandmother was alive she would tell him he'd been like that from childhood. Fussing whenever she was out of sight. It made sense, since immediately after giving birth, his mother had overdosed on heroine, leaving him cold and hungry, squalling next to her lifeless body.

His early teens had been difficult. He was a scrawny, sickly kid who didn't make connections quickly. But once the band got together and grew in popularity, it became increasingly easier to surround himself with people. Women, friends, wanna-be friends—it didn't matter. He was a gypsy, just as Becca claimed. Moving from city to city, country to country, and friend's guest room to friend's guest room so as never to be alone. At least not physically.

But damnit, he was tired of it. He wanted a sense of belonging, a sense of permanence. Being a wanderer no longer appealed. Instead, he longed to feel as if he'd made an impact on life. Like he'd done something important. The music had been enough for a while, but now he desired so much more.

Too bad he had no idea how to get it.

Setting his bass in the stand, Dominic ran his fingers down the neck. An Ibanez six-string with a gorgeous alder body and maple top – his most prized possession. One of few. He'd learned a long time ago that possessions could be lost or taken away, so it was best not to have any. Not anything that really mattered. The more it mattered, the greater the need to keep his distance.

Which was the root of his problem. Pulling his mobile from his pocket, he scrolled through the gallery until he found the photo he wanted. The one that showed the most beautiful woman he'd ever known, smiling up at him from his own bed.

Rebecca.

She had mattered to him. More than he'd dare admit. He'd run from her, not because of the words she'd spoken, but because he'd been tempted to say them back. Childhood fears were the most difficult to eradicate. Even now they had the power to reach out and grab him by the throat. Three years ago when his feelings were so raw and new to him…he'd never stood a chance.

Damn it. He closed his eyes and shook his head, as the need to escape surged, grew strong enough he couldn't ignore it. However, acknowledging the need didn't mean he had to follow through with it. No, there had to be something else that could be done. This is one thing in his life that was worth fighting for. The other things, not so much, so it was easy to let them go. Not Becca. He loved her too much to stand by and do nothing. He had to make things right between them.

Clueless as to how to go about it, he glanced at the ceiling of the studio and wondered.

****

"So, you *do* want to work things out with her?" Isabeau asked. "Because, we've talked about this before and still you never called her. I take it staring down a semi and winning made you realize something was missing?"

Maybe this wasn't such a good idea after all. Dominic had come up from the basement looking for a woman's point of view. He'd wanted to speak with Isa alone, but instead found her and Noah together in the oversized lounge chair that fit the two of them perfectly. Noah's arm was around her, Isabeau leaning against him as much as the chair back. "I knew something was missing before the accident," he admitted. "But seeing her again...cemented it."

Isabeau smiled, effectively but silently telling him she was pleased. "You want Rebecca, go get her."

He rolled his eyes. "Wow, thanks. I've never heard that before."

"What do you want me to say?"

"Tell me...I don't bloody know! Tell me the secret."

She looked up at him with a confused stare that failed to reassure. "What secret? What makes you think I know a secret?"

Dominic gestured to the chair, the two of them sitting as one. Connected. "*This* secret! How do I get to this?" Honestly, it was a little painful to look at them. "You two...you make it seem so easy."

"Sure, it's easy now, but getting here? You were there with us, how can you think it was easy?" Isabeau scooted to the front edge of the chair, separating herself from Noah, moving closer to the couch where Dominic sat. "Dom, you shared things with me once, things I don't think you've ever shared with anyone before. About your childhood fears."

She went straight for the jugular, didn't she?

"Why did you tell me? Why me?"

He'd wanted to tell someone. As a way to let loose, to exorcise the demons in his head that never let up. Never went away no matter the passage of time. Why he'd chosen her, remained a mystery. "I don't know."

"Yes, you do. It wasn't that I'm safe. I could leave you, just like everyone else in your life has done at one time or another, even Noah."

Dominic opened his mouth, prepared to defend his friend, then shut it. Noah had left him. At a time when he'd needed him most.

Noah startled. "I've never—"

"Yes you did, Noah," Isabeau said, cutting off his argument. "After Danny died. You didn't plan to, but you did, you left them all. Didn't he, Dominic? He abandoned the band. He abandoned *you*."

"Jesus," Noah muttered.

Shit. This wasn't the conversation Dom had in mind when he'd searched out Isabeau tonight.

"You wanted to trust someone," she said, her expression softening along with her tone. "You wanted to trust me, so you did. I love you, Dom, like the brother I always wanted. But the person you need to open up to is Rebecca."

All he could do was stare at her, his thoughts in a whirl.

"I know what you're running from. I also know you're tired of running." He was. God, he was. "So, stop. Stop running, please. You want what Noah and I have, and you deserve it. But you can't have it, you'll never have it, until you stop running and talk to her. Trust her, Dom."

He was just a musician who'd clawed his way out of the shit he'd been born in. Rebecca was smart, educated, with a good job, good breeding and a family. She deserved a guy who stayed in one place, with a home, a career, stability. She deserved the white picket fence.

He wasn't that guy. He didn't know how to be that guy. "Becca deserves better than me."

"Dominic Parker Price!" Isabeau's eyes lit with anger. "How dare you! What about you makes you not worthy? Your big heart? Your capacity to love?"

He clawed his fingers through his hair. "You don't know what I said to her."

"That's the past. You can't change the past no matter how much you may want to. You know that. I know that. Noah knows that. All that matters is what you say to her now. What will you say to her?"

Good goddamn question. "There's nothing I can say that will change what I did to her. She told me to go away."

She pressed her lips into a tight line and frowned. "How long ago was this? You didn't listen did you?"

"A week ago."

Isabeau sighed.

"She told me to go away," he repeated.

"Do you have any idea how many times I told Noah to go away?"

"At least three," Noah piped up.

152

She nodded. "He never listened. Why did you?"

"That's different," Dom argued.

"How is it different?" Isabeau wanted to know.

"You loved Noah. You didn't really mean it."

"Oh, she meant it." Noah argued.

"Seriously?" Dominic asked, even though he could tell Noah was telling the truth. "Women don't make any sense."

Isabeau chuffed. "And men do?" She stared at Dom without commenting further. Long enough that he began to squirm. Then she smiled that knowing feminine smile he'd seen so many women wear. "Is this how you feel when pointing out the obvious to me?"

Dom stacked his hands atop his head. "What are you talking about?"

"What exactly did she say to you?"

Go away, Dominic. "I'd rather not—"

"Dominic."

"She told me to go away, okay? And..." *Shit.* The pain was worse than he imagined. He pushed the heel of his palm into his chest and rubbed.

"And?"

I don't love you anymore, Dominic.

"What else did she say?" Isabeau prodded.

"That she doesn't love me anymore." The words tore from his throat all jagged edges and bitter taste, but it was better to get them out

153

before they strangled him.

"Why?"

"Why what?"

"Why did she tell you that?"

He released a long breath. "Because I'm a bloody bastard!"

"Why else?"

Dom propped his elbows on his knees and pushed his hair away from his face. Once he spoke them aloud, Rebecca's words circled his mind like a vulture.

"Isabeau," Noah warned. "Put the poor man out of his misery. He's not going to get there on his own. He's too close to the situation."

I don't love you anymore, Dominic. Goddamnit, could her haunting words not let up for five fucking seconds?

"He's an intelligent man," she argued. "He'll see it."

"What the hell are you talking about?" The only thing Dominic saw was Becca's face; the pain in her eyes as she told him she didn't love him. Over and over it played through his mind, leaving him raw and bleeding. "Just spill it, will you?"

Isabeau blinked. "Still cranky, I see."

Surging to his feet, Dominic headed for the door. He pulled it open with a violent twist of the handle.

"You went to see her, didn't you?" Isabeau asked, her voice soft and full of understanding.

He waited with his hand on the door as she crossed to him. "It wasn't the first time you showed up on her doorstep, was it?"

"No."

"The first couple of times she was civil – maybe you talked a bit, even laughed." He turned his head slowly and looked at her. "But the last time something was different, wasn't it?"

How the hell does she know this?

She touched his arm. "What did she say to you, Dominic?"

It was easier to gaze out into the darkness than look at Isabeau as he said the words. Vocalized them, because he was tired of keeping them to himself. "She said I'd been content without her for years. That how was she to believe I felt any differently when it took an accident to get me to come back to her."

"What else?"

"Fuck, Isa," he mumbled and scrubbed the back of his neck. Reliving this was like ripping his heart out a second time. "She said she'd never said the words before."

"I love you," she whispered.

His gut tightened as a hollowness settled in his chest. He shook his head, thumped his fist against the doorframe. "Yes. And what did I do? I ran all the way back to London. I threw it away – what we had – what we could have been."

"Because you got scared."

"*Yes.*" Of three little words. Of an emotion so foreign to him that he didn't know how to deal with it. But mostly, of ending up alone. Which he had anyway.

"Ironic, isn't it?"

"What?"

"You're both afraid of the same thing, just for different reasons."

With a sigh he returned his gaze to her, feeling like he'd just gone to the battlefield but hadn't necessarily won the war. "I have no idea what you're talking about."

"Now it's Rebecca who's scared. Don't you see it? Dominic, after all the time that has passed, the only way you walking out still hurts her is if she still cares for you."

He blinked. "But she *told* me to go."

"To save herself the pain. Better you leave her now than later, when there's even more memories to haunt her."

"Who said I'll leave her?"

"She *knows* you'll leave her, Dom. The same way I knew Noah would leave me."

He could only stare at her as everything clicked into place. "Right up until the moment he proposed."

"*Yes.*" She flashed him a grin that quickly faded. "Only instead of proving Rebecca wrong by staying, you proved her right."

"The hell I did!" He stepped out the door,

then back in. Feeling as if he'd lost about a hundred pounds from around his neck, he grabbed Isabeau by the shoulders and planted a kiss on her mouth.

"Hey! Go get your own!" Noah yelled as Dominic sprinted out the door and to his car.

CHAPTER TWELVE

Rebecca pulled into her driveway to find Dominic leaning against the post of the front porch. It'd been a lousy week and the last thing she needed, the last possible thing she could deal with right now, was him. Yet here he was. Looking as sinfully gorgeous as ever.

His long black hair was messy, like he'd been running his fingers through it. Her own twitched with the need to bury her hands in his hair and pull him to her. Pull him in tight, setting aside everything that stood between them. Trusting this time would be different.

For a long moment the temptation was so great she couldn't breathe. She walked past him, used her key to unlock the door but didn't open it. Exhaustion pulled at her, made her limbs heavy and her eyes burn. The double shift she'd just come off had been difficult, made more so by the arrival of Mr. Masters – the little boy's father. He hadn't said anything, just stood against a light pole outside the emergency entrance. In a fashion eerily similar to the way Dominic stood now.

It had taken her the entire drive home to

shake off the trickle of alarm from between her shoulder blades.

Unable to summon the most basic of manners, she sighed. "Not tonight, Dom." Tonight she felt far too exposed and vulnerable. "Honestly, I don't have the strength for another go around with you."

He looked her over slowly, studying her without a word. She knew what she looked like, had seen her reflection in the mirror after getting cleaned up at the hospital. Dark circles of fatigue beneath bloodshot eyes, her naturally pale skin more drawn than normal. She couldn't hold her tongue when she was tired. No doubt he'd use that to his advantage.

"Are you okay?"

The fact that he asked, after everything they'd said to each other, nearly brought tears to her eyes. *No.* "Yes."

He was quiet a moment, then blew out a breath. "I was hoping to have that talk you wanted, but I can see tonight's not the night."

She allowed herself to relax a bit. "It's really not."

"Just so you know, I'll go home tonight, but I'm not going away."

"What does that mean?"

Dominic gazed deep into her eyes. "I want a second chance, Rebecca." His tone was a dark promise that curled around her and had her pulse kicking hard. "A chance to show you how much I've changed. To be what you want me to be; a lover *and* a friend."

Heart in her throat she could only whisper. "For how long?"

"As long as you'll have me."

She closed her eyes and swallowed back the ache, the longing. *Yes*, cried her heart. *Oh please, yes.* Her head refused to believe. "Dom," she murmured.

He didn't speak. Nor did he walk away. Instead, he stepped closer. So close his breath brushed her temple, his body heat warmed her. She opened her eyes, tipped her head up to see into his. He stood close enough to touch her, only he didn't. "Your best friend's name is Karmen."

Confusion scattered her thoughts. "How?"

"You're wrong. I met her once – the same night I met you. She's Latina, pretty but...I barely remember her." His eyes darkened to mirror the night sky. "I was too blinded by you."

"Dominic." She lifted a hand and settled it in the center of his chest, feeling the hard muscle as well as the heat—traced her fingers over one pec and his body tightened.

Still, he didn't touch her.

"You listen to classical music all the time. So much it used to drive me bonkers. But only if you're happy. When you're sad, you listen to the blues."

Or his. She'd grown quite fond of Black

Phoenix's music over the years.

"I don't recall what make or model your car was, just that it was a bit dodgy and smelled like cheese." His chuckle vibrated up her arm.

God, how was she supposed to resist this? He was giving her everything she'd demanded of him the other night. All the answers she'd accused him of not caring enough to have. Rebecca leaned in, pressing closer, absorbing his scent, his proximity, and still his arms remained at his sides. He wasn't going to make it easy on her. Anything that might happen, everything was being left up to her.

"I had a kink in my ass for a week after that first night." His gaze fell to hers as she laughed. "I would do anything to make you laugh." His voice was low, raw, as he reverently touched her cheek. "I would do anything to make sure I never make you cry again. I don't want to be what makes you cry, Rebecca. Not anymore."

Her body wouldn't stop shaking. "Dominic."

"I miss you so much. I miss us. There's not a day goes by that I don't regret walking away from you."

It was too much to take in at once. Rebecca couldn't move, and her vocal cords seemed to be temporarily useless. She ended up just standing there, as her heart took a hard leap against her ribs and hope blossomed.

"I wanted you to know that." His gaze remained on hers as he took a step back. "You look knackered. Get some sleep."

A chill worked through her as the distance between them grew. She shook her head as unaccustomed desperation welled up inside her. "Wait," she said breathlessly, even as her head told her heart not to risk again.

He waited. For her to say something. For her to continue.

She fought for breath, for courage. She wanted him. His touch. His kiss. She had to have both. She would worry about regrets later. With a deep breath for courage, Rebecca made the conscious decision not to live in fear of tomorrow. Instead, she listened to her heart, and trusted Dominic. "How's your headache?"

Confusion furrowed his brow. "My headache? Better, I hardly notice it anymore."

"Good," she said with a nod. Then, before she could talk herself out of it, she grabbed a fistful of his shirt, stepped closer, and pressed her mouth against his.

He froze for the space of a heartbeat then it was as if a dam burst. He buried his hands in her hair, held her in place while he took over, possessing her in a hard, wet kiss.

She gave herself over to the sensation of him. His taste, his scent, the heat of his body. The way his hands flexed and opened as he cupped the back of her head and came at her from a different angle.

It went on, long and hot, deep and wet. He

pinned her to her front door and kissed her until her worry faded, until her bones began to liquefy. He kissed her until nothing else existed but him. It was like coming home after being away for an extended vacation.

"Rebecca," he murmured against her mouth.

God how she'd missed this: his touch, his taste, his scent. He slid his thigh between hers, and Rebecca gasped and rocked against it. He released a low, rough sound of hunger then dropped a hand from her hair to her ass, squeezing, pulling her closer, so she rode up his leg. Pleasure crashed over her. She squirmed, trying to get even closer. She'd have crawled right into him if she could. "Tell me you want this, Rebecca."

He had to ask? She was gripping his shirt in both fists, and riding his leg like a mechanical bull. The friction was sweet, but it wasn't enough. "I want this."

He ran his mouth over her jaw to her ear while he let go of her hair, sliding his free hand down her back to cup her bottom, until he held a cheek in each palm. Lifting her off his leg, he opened her up so that as he pressed into her again, he slid his erection directly against her core. "Tell me."

Oh, God. She shook her head and clutched him. A shuddery breath escaped. "I want you, Dominic. Take me inside, throw me on the bed, and fuck me until I scream."

With a sound that was nearly a growl he crushed his mouth to hers, his tongue delving deep. The door swung open, and for a moment she feared he would drop her. But his hands remained firm and steady and the moment passed. Without missing a step or taking his tongue out of her mouth, he pushed it closed then strode down the hall to her bedroom.

Just inside the doorway, he slowly let her slide down his body until she stood on her own two feet. "I want to see you." The rough timbre of his voice made her shiver. "I need to see you."

She flipped the switch, then blinked as she adjusted to the light.

He traced his fingertips over her cheek, her jaw, down the front of her throat to the vee of her blouse. Her breath backed up as one by one he worked her buttons open, exposing her pale pink bra. "Look at you," he murmured, pushing the shirt off her shoulders. Her nipples hardened. She shivered, and it wasn't because she was cold.

His eyes were bright, and he was having trouble breathing, same as her. He brushed her long hair off her shoulder and bent to kiss her collarbone, drew on a patch of skin and sucked, as he dragged his thumb over the swell of her breast.

If he hadn't been supporting her, Rebecca was certain she would have melted into a puddle on the floor.

"Take it off, Becca," he commanded, his lips brushing over the shell of her ear.

She shook her head. "You first."

He stared at her, his expression nearly violent with need, color high on his cheeks. With one arm, he ripped his cotton shirt over his head and flung it on the floor. Toeing off his shoes, he kicked them aside, then his hands were at his waist, working the zipper on his jeans and pushing them off his hips. His erection jutted out, smooth, long and thick.

Rebecca swallowed roughly, arousal making it hard to breathe. Reaching behind her back, she unhooked her bra, cupping the material to her breasts as the straps slid down her arms.

His nostrils flared.

She let it fall to the floor.

He moved his gaze over her, lingering, caressing, scorching her skin, before stopping at her waist. "The rest," he rasped.

With a last look in his eyes she peeled off her slacks and panties, turning from him and bending over to remove her shoes at the same time. The sound he made gave her a heady rush. His warm hands settled on her hips, his fingers pressing into her skin as he pulled her back against him.

"Oh, God, Dom." She straightened so their bodies were flush, the front of him against the back of her. He went still a minute, then swore savagely as she rocked her ass against his erection. His grip on her hips tightened and suddenly she was airborne, as he threw her on the bed.

She landed face up with barely enough time to catch her breath before he grasped her ankles and parted her legs, exposing her, all of her, to his gaze. His breathing quickened. His eyes darkened as he looked at her. Slowly. Taking his time. She was comfortable in her own skin, but his intense, intimate examination made her squirm.

"Becca," he sighed, his voice so low she barely heard it. "I never thought I'd get to see you like this again."

The bed dipped beneath his weight as he settled onto his knees between her legs. Calloused fingertips skimmed up her thighs, over her hips and higher. His gaze followed as he slid his fingers farther north, circling her nipples, stroking and toying with them. He cupped her right breast and plumped it. "Fuck, I love your body," he said huskily. Then he lowered his head and took her nipple into his mouth.

Already half gone, she cried out. She stroked his hair, reveling in its soft, silky strands, the way it brushed against her skin. As arousing as his mouth. Unable to hold still, she fisted her hands in his hair and pulled him close at the same time as she arched her back.

He groaned his approval, then switched to

her other breast, taking his time kissing, licking and sucking at her flesh. The pleasure was torturous. He dragged his hand downward, tracing a path over her ribs, her stomach before slipping into her curls. "You are so wet," he growled, penetrating her with his fingers. "So hot and wet." She exhaled on a sharp gasp of pleasure, trembling slightly at the hot rush his touch set off.

He fingered her slow, mimicking the act they raced toward. Tension built inside her, tied her in a knot of pleasure so tight she wanted to scream with the need to untie it. She dug her fingers into his shoulders as she pushed against his hand, half out of her mind. "Dom," she whispered, on the edge, the very edge, and when he responded by adding his thumb, tapping out a rhythm against her clit, she exploded.

She dug her heels into the mattress and arched her back as his name echoed off her bedroom walls.

"Easy, beautiful, we're just getting started." Sliding down her body, he pushed her legs up toward her chest, opening her even further, and dragged his tongue through her folds. He was relentless, using his tongue, his teeth, then his oh-so talented fingers. Arousal shot through her once more, and even though she'd just come so hard she thought she couldn't do it again, he proved her wrong.

She moaned and thrashed beneath him, his

hand on her stomach holding her down as he continued to lick and suck, not stopping until her body went limp. It was a moment before she drifted back to her senses. She heard him tear open a condom, and when she opened her eyes, he had his forearms on either side of her head and was gazing into her face. She touched his jaw, his mouth, sighing in pleasure as he pushed into her.

"Becca, God, you feel incredible," he whispered, pressing a kiss to her lips. It was an erotic rush, tasting her own juices. "I almost forgot how it feels to be inside a woman. It's so much better than my fist."

She laughed. He clenched his hands lightly in her hair as he released a sound that was a cross between a laugh and a groan. A sound that vibrated throughout her entire body, sparking her desire. Her nipples tightened. Her sex pulsed.

"Don't do that," he grated out. "As it is I won't last more than sixty seconds."

She knew his stamina to be incredible. He could bring her to climax more times than she could count before succumbing to the pleasure. He had, on more than one occasion. "I'm betting you can last a bit longer than that." Rebecca squeezed her pelvic muscles.

He let out another rough sound, this one completely void of humor. "Don't."

"Don't bet or don't do that again?" She tilted

her pelvis up and squeezed again.

He growled low in his throat.

Realizing how close to the edge he really was sent a thrill of feminine pleasure through her, made her feel powerful. *She* was doing this to him, making him lose control.

She slid her hands over his back and lower, cupping his ass and pulling him deeper into her as she tightened around his length. Beneath her palms his hard muscles bunched and flexed just before his body began to shake. His hold on her hair tightened as he struggled for control. A battle he lost as he began to move in quick, pounding thrusts, and came with a guttural shout.

His whole body went loose. He dropped his forehead to the bed beside hers and muttered, "Bloody hell, that's embarrassing."

Rebecca trailed her fingertips down the indent of his spine, relishing every twitch and flex along the way. "You know, as a physician I could help you with your—"

"Don't you dare."

"—condition. There are tricks you can use to—" Her words turned to a squeal as he rolled her, then to laughter even as he misjudged and they landed in a heap on the floor.

His breath left him in a whoosh as he cushioned her fall.

"Dom?"

It was a moment before he seemed to breathe

again.

"Dominic? Are you okay?"

"I might need your medical license after all," he groaned.

His ribs!

Rebecca sat up, immediately concerned. He was no longer wrapping them, but that didn't mean the fall hadn't angered the injury. She moved her hands over his torso, doing her best to assess his condition. The bruise on his side had faded away. He didn't show any signs of tenderness when she pressed his ribs. Switching to his arms, she smoothed her hands up, her fingers brushing over the sutures on his left upper arm.

"Shit. If you pulled your..." she stopped. "Why do you still have sutures? You should have had them removed already."

He rubbed the back of his head. "I trigger faster than a fifteen year old copping his first feel, then follow it up by knocking a few brain cells loose and all you're concerned about is my arm?"

Rebecca looked down at him, really looked this time, and was surprised by what she found. "You have nothing to be embarrassed about." Being wanted so fiercely was damn sexy. She couldn't think of anything sexier. "Let me get these sutures out, and I'll give you another chance to prove your virility."

"How about I redeem myself first, and *then*

you can worry about the bloody sutures?" he growled, then rolled her beneath him and did exactly that.

****

Rebecca came awake suddenly, remaining still as she waited for her mind to grab hold of what had pulled her from slumber. The heat was the first thing she noted, emanating from the man spooned against her back. Dominic. They were on her bed, naked, having succumbed to exhaustion after their second – correction third – round of lovemaking. Skin to skin, one of his legs thrown over both of hers, there was no need for bed coverings. Which was good since they all seemed to be missing.

Dom's breathing was even, his heart rhythm normal against her back. So what...? Then she felt it. The gentle slap of his thumb against her hip.

Memory reached up and grabbed her by the throat. Of the other nights spent lying in his arms. Other times she'd woken in the middle of the night in wonder. The first night, and how it had taken her a while to figure out what he was doing.

For a moment she lay still, as his thumb continued to tap. She didn't question how even after the years they'd been apart, the action seemed so familiar. Or why it brought a calm to her world. Instead, she linked her fingers with his and drifted back to sleep.

CHAPTER THIRTEEN

Dominic stood facing the shower, arms out before him, braced on the tile, head bent so the water beat down on his shoulders and neck. His headache was back, lack of sleep the most likely cause. Then again bouncing his skull off the floor last night probably didn't help. He'd take the pain though, if it meant a repeat of what had come after.

He'd had his merry way with Becca on the floor where they'd landed. Then again in the bathroom, where after removing his sutures, he'd taken her from behind as she'd held onto the vanity for support. It was the most erotic encounter of his life, the mirror reflecting the flush of her skin, sway of her breasts, and sparkle of excitement in her green eyes as she focused on the image of his cock sliding in and out of her channel.

Christ. He'd never be able to look at a mirror the same way again.

A flick of his wrist turned the water temperature to cold. Even that didn't help the ache of arousal. The shower gel smelled like her so now he smelled like her. Smelled like her and had the image of her coming apart in this very room burned into his brain.

Turning off the water, he towel dried and pulled on his Levis, heading out of the bedroom in search of Rebecca. There was just enough time for an encore before he had to be in Auburn.

He found her in the kitchen, back to him, wearing hip-hugging jeans and a green tee. Rebecca. In jeans. For a minute Dominic forgot to breathe.

When they'd been together she'd never worn jeans. Dress slacks and blouses, skirt and blazers—professional women's wear. Never jeans. She hadn't even owned a pair. Especially not a pair that hugged her curves like they'd been made with her in mind, a faded blue, worn white at the seams.

He opened his mouth to comment, then realized she was talking on the phone.

"I can't come to dinner tonight, I have other plans."

Damn straight she did.

"No, not with a man. You know I'm not...seeing anyone right now."

The hell she wasn't.

Stepping up behind her, Dom pressed a kiss to her temple, while reaching around her to snag the mug of coffee from her hand. He made sure to brush as much of himself against her as possible, knowing she couldn't mistake the bulge of his erection. "Morning, beautiful."

She shivered visibly then faced him as he leaned against the counter, turning the mug to place his lips over the stain of lipstick she'd left. Her eyes flashed, then softened.

"Yes, that was a man," she said, closing her eyes and pinching the bridge of her nose. "No, it's not Nathan."

There was that name again—*Nathan*.

"I know, mom," she sighed, then held out her hand, gesturing at the mug.

Not a big fan of coffee, he passed it back to her, making sure their fingers brushed during the hand off. He couldn't help himself.

"I know. Mom..." She stared up at him as she sipped her coffee. "Because I didn't wish to have this conversation with you." She made a face, eyes crossed, tongue peeking out of her mouth and he laughed aloud. "Yes, he has a very nice laugh. He has a lot of very nice qualities." She eyed his naked chest. "No, you can't meet him just yet. Why? Because you'll start talking grandbabies and scare him away, that's why!"

Dom sighed, having to shake his head. *Grandbabies? Jesus.*

"See what you did, Mom? You've put the look of panic in his eyes. We'll talk about this later, okay? I love you, too." Rebecca set her cell phone on the counter next to him and dropped her forehead to his chest. "You've started something now," she murmured wearily.

175

He slid a hand beneath her hair, massaging her neck at the base of her skull. She responded with a moan that spread heat across his flesh and gripped his lower belly in a white, hot fist.

Her free hand settled on his chest, fingers swirling, drawing patterns in the hair. "She's going to start calling every day, asking when she can meet you."

He pulled her closer and nuzzled just beneath her ear. "And that's bad?"

"Are you serious? That's terrible!" She sucked in a breath, then let it out slowly as he slid his free hand down her back to settle on her denim-covered ass. "Next thing you know she'll begin naming our children."

He laughed softly. "As long as she doesn't go for any sissy names."

"Dominic."

"Hmmm?" He kissed her jaw, her mouth.

She pushed back a little and stared up at him. "I can't believe this doesn't bother you."

"I can't believe it *does* bother you." Mothers were supposed to do things like that. Weren't they?

"You don't know—"

Unable to resist any longer, he kissed her, cutting off her flow of words. He'd meant for it to help convince her to remove her clothes, but he couldn't shake loose the question niggling his brain. "Who's Nathan?"

A wordless plea of protest slipped from her

lips as she curled her fingers into his pec. "Wh-what?"

"You've mentioned him twice."

Rebecca blinked up at him. After placing her mug on the counter, she sank against him from chest to knee. "He's nobody."

"Bec—"

Surging up, she covered his mouth with hers.

As distractions went, it was a good one. She was sweet, so damn sweet. Her soft curves molded to him as if she were made for him. She ran her hands ran over him everywhere she could reach. For a moment he gave into her, drinking her in with a low, rough groan. "Stop." Hands on her upper arms he pushed her back a step but didn't let go.

A shiver worked through her body as she stared at his mouth like she wanted more. "Why?"

Because if he didn't stop her he was going to remove her clothes and take her on the edge of the counter. Which he couldn't do. Not with the expert way she'd evaded his question, leaving him in the dark as to Nathan's identity. He stared down at her, waiting. She was a smart woman, smart enough to know what he was waiting for.

She took a breath as if she was going to speak, then her gaze drifted away, settling somewhere over his left shoulder.

His heart skipped a beat. "Fuck." He

released her arms, shoving his hands in his pockets. "You said you weren't seeing anyone."

"My mother gets ideas—"

"The other night, Rebecca, when *I* asked you. You told me you weren't seeing anyone."

She gave him a bemused look. "I'm not. We...dated, but that was a while back."

He released a pent up breath, stacking both hands atop his head. For a moment there he'd thought he was poaching, or at the very least had competition. "You could have just said that."

"I just did."

He shook his head in frustration, then started for the bedroom.

"Where are you going?" she asked his back.

"To finish dressing. We have to be at brunch by eleven-thirty and I want to swing by my place for a clean shirt first."

"Your place? I thought you were staying with Noah and Isabeau? And why do you assume I'll go with you? Maybe I have other plans."

Spinning, he closed the distance between them in three strides. He curved his hand around the back of her neck and pulled her close. "Cancel them," he said, his voice harsh even to his own ears. "You're going with me, Rebecca, because I said I would be there." Damnit, he needed to calm down, but all the talk of her dating other people was driving him batshit crazy. Combine that with the low pulse of arousal that heated his blood whenever she was near and he was like a powder keg, primed and ready to go off. He took a deep breath, trying against all odds to regain composure. "I want you with me, so I can introduce you to my friends." His family. "I think you'll like them. That way everyone knows this Nathan character is out of the picture."

She placed a hand on his chest. "Dom—"

"Then I'm going to toss you on the nearest bed, and..." Leaning down he made sure his lips brushed her ear as he told her in blunt, graphic detail what he planned to do to her even as he went rock hard at the thought.

"Holy mother of God," she whimpered. "I'll get my shoes."

****

"I'm not saying anything, Dom," Rebecca said to his broad back as he used his key to lock his apartment door. "It's a cute little place."

"Cute being a code word for what, exactly?"

He was acting like it was a dirty word. Or at the very least, a word that didn't belong in the male vernacular. If it wasn't so much fun seeing him riled up over the apartment, she may have taken pity on him. Instead, she was planning how she could use the word to describe him. If he thought describing his apartment as cute was bad...

She smiled.

He raised an eyebrow. "Are you messing with me, Becca?" he asked, stuffing the key in his pocket.

The action drew her attention to his hands. God, his fingers. She already knew the skill of those ten digits, and the pleasure they could bring. The things he'd promised to do with them later...just thinking about it brought a warm flush to her face. "Maybe."

Immediately, his gaze homed in on her cheeks. "Maybe?" He paused, considering her a moment. "Are you blushing?"

"Of course not." Even if she didn't have skin that gave away her secrets, she'd never been any good at lying.

He flashed a smile. The one that always made her want to take all her clothes off. "You going to share?"

"Share what?"

"What you're thinking about that has you blushing."

The warmth in her cheeks kicked up a notch.

So did his smile. "I'm going to like this, aren't I?" he said, voice husky.

"What makes you so sure it has anything to do with you?" she asked, a bit too breathlessly for her liking.

His smile turned to laughter. Lines creased the corners of his eyes.

Rebecca shook her head and turned away. What else could she do? She was halfway down the outside steps that led to his apartment when she stopped. "What time did you say we were supposed to be there?"

He didn't answer. A glance over her shoulder found him still smiling, an unreadable look in his eye.

"I like how you said 'we'."

Did she? She hadn't noticed.

"Eleven-thirty. Why?"

"Because I'm fairly certain that's Isabeau in the alley across the street."

He looked past her, surprise on his face.

"There," she said, pointing. "Near that young girl."

"Come on." He slipped around her and led her down the stairs, settling a hand at her lower back as he glanced in both directions and crossed the street.

The young girl in question had long dark brown hair, parted in the middle and styled into two braids down her back. She wore a navy zip-front hoodie over a sapphire blue Henley, jeans torn at the knees, and canvas shoes with no laces. She carried an army green backpack that looked like it'd come from a surplus store, hands fisted so tightly on the strap her knuckles were white.

Rebecca curled her fingers around Dominic's bicep. "Hold up. Give her some space."

"Isabeau?"

"The girl." She was favoring her right side,

181

her breaths shallow and too fast. Concern caused Rebecca to take another step in their direction. A move that spooked the child.

In the blink of an eye, she was gone.

Isabeau sighed. She pressed her fingers to her lips, her attention focused on the spot the girl had stood. Then she started down the alley.

She was about ten feet from them when Dominic spoke, "Isabeau?"

She jerked and faced them, surprise written all over her face. "I didn't see you there, I'm...sorry."

Dom studied her a moment. "We're running late, which means you're superbly late. To your own gathering."

Isabeau flashed a smile. "I needed something from the market."

"Yeah?" He paused, then tipped his head in the direction Isabeau had just come. "Was that her?"

Rebecca straightened. His reference spoke of a prior knowledge of the young girl. If he knew her, perhaps he knew how she'd been injured. More importantly, whether or not she'd received medical attention. It didn't take a Ph.D. to figure out the girl was in trouble.

"Her name is Chloe," Isabeau said.

"So, she told you her name. That's good, right?" Dom flicked a glance at Rebecca, as if making sure she remained a part of the conversation. "Did you invite Chloe to lunch?"

Isabeau let out a deep breath. "No. She doesn't trust me yet."

"That's understandable," he replied softly.

"Yes it is." She shifted her attention off Dominic and focused on Rebecca. "Good morning, Rebecca. You look positively radiant this morning."

"Subtle," Dominic said before Rebecca could reply. "I take it we're done talking about your new friend?"

"What?" she asked innocently, then ruined it by laughing. "Maybe I'm just interested in getting to know *your* new friend. She is glowing though. You are glowing," she told Rebecca.

"Thank you," Rebecca replied with a smile. "As are you."

"Wow, this isn't uncomfortable at all," Dominic said drolly.

Isabeau's eyebrow arched.

Rebecca shook her head. "Don't worry; he thinks everything is code this morning."

"Yeah?"

"I called his apartment cute."

She grinned. "It is nice, isn't it?"

"Now it's cute *and* nice?" Dominic looked absolutely horrified by the thought. "Fantastic."

Rebecca slipped her hand into his, a broad smile on her face. She patted his bicep with her free hand, then gave it a squeeze, distracted for a moment by the play of muscle beneath her fingers. "So, you don't like the word cute, how

183

about quaint? Is quaint better?"

"Quaint is a nice word," Isabeau agreed.

Dominic stared at Rebecca, his eyes flashing. "You drive me crazy."

"Good."

He didn't reply, just continued to look at her, torn between amusement and frustration. She wanted to forget they had plans and kiss that frustration away. Drag him back across the street, up those stairs and into his quaint apartment, peeling off his clothes along the way.

At just the thought, her hand involuntarily squeezed his bicep.

His eyes dilated.

Isabeau cleared her throat. "I have to get back to the house, so…" She motioned down the street, where her crossover sat at the curb.

"Right," Dom said. "We'll walk you to your car."

"I think I can manage." She took a few steps, walking backward. "I guess I'll see you guys…later."

"We'll be right behind you," Rebecca assured her, ignoring the niggle of regret that she had to reign in her desire.

CHAPTER FOURTEEN

If Rebecca had to use one word to describe brunch at Isabeau and Noah's it would be chaotic. Also surprisingly organized and *fun*.

Which proved there was no way to describe it in one word. How could she begin to? Musicians and their families, gathered around a table covered with more food than they could possibly eat in one sitting, joking and laughing like the loudest, albeit oddest, family she could ever imagine.

Just walking into the house had been an adventure. They'd barely stepped inside before the squeals of children and echoes of feet running on the hardwood floors hit them. Someone hollered about a dog then, sure enough, a barking ball of fluff rounded the corner, aiming for Rebecca and the freedom of the open door behind her. Hot on the pup's tail came a young boy so intent on the chase, he appeared oblivious to the impending crash.

She managed to close the door in time, causing the pup to skid to a stop – or try to. The dog hit the brakes, paws slipping and sliding so that he skidded between her legs and smacked into the door. The boy wasn't having better luck stopping. She braced for impact when Dominic reached out with one arm, snatching the boy off the ground.

He ruffled the child's unruly mop of chocolate brown hair. "Hello David, still struggling to control that hairball? You don't get yours cut soon, you're going to start looking like the mutt."

The mutt was actually a long-haired German Shepard if she wasn't mistaken. Who, now that the door was closed, was jumping and nipping at his boy's dangling feet.

"Look who's talking," David said, giving Dom's hair a tug and causing Rebecca to laugh out loud.

Two sets of male eyes turned in her direction.

David tipped his head closer to Dominic's. "Who's that?" he whispered loud enough she was certain the people in the other room heard him.

"That's Rebecca."

He squinted like he was really checking her out, and she had to stifle another laugh. If she had to guess she'd place his age around seven or eight. "She's got hair like a carrot," he stated, still in that pseudo-whisper.

"I suppose she does."

"I like carrots."

Dom choked out a laugh.

Wiggling to get loose, David took off again

the moment his feet hit the floor, and this time the puppy gave chase.

"Cute kid," Rebecca said, smiling at the boy's retreating back.

"That was David. He's Nick and Tracey's boy."

Hadn't Isabeau mentioned them the other day? "Nick's the band's...guitarist."

"He is."

A tiny girl of about four stepped into the entry, green eyes too big for her face focused on Dominic. He flashed her the softest smile Rebecca had ever seen, then promptly scooped her up when she lifted her arms to him.

"This little beauty is Katie."

"And she is...?"

"Also Nick and Tracey's."

"Hi, Katie."

Katie averted her eyes, and lifted her fisted hand toward her mouth, thumb sticking out like a straw. Dom intercepted the move with a skill that spoke of practice, his hand shifting to her back when she buried her face in his neck. "Katie is a bit bashful."

Rebecca found the ease in which he dealt with both children very interesting. It was a side of him she wouldn't have expected. He was just so beautiful. The black hair and blue eyes, his olive skin. He oozed testosterone at levels high enough that women went a little crazy around him. Her included. Add his career choice into that mix, the fact that his life was tour buses, concert halls and screaming fans? She'd honestly never imagined he could be so comfortable around children and puppies and...family.

"Becca?"

"Hmm...what?"

He was still holding Katie, and even though he was looking at Rebecca, he managed to intercept her thumb a second time. "You're not thinking of making a run for it, are you?" A hint of humor flashed across his face.

"Why would you say that?" Maybe it wasn't fair to have made such assumptions about him, but honestly, how could she have known?

"You're looking a little shell-shocked and we haven't even gotten to the scary stuff yet."

Oh, she begged to differ. She'd never seen anything more terrifying than the man who stood before her right now. He'd been hard enough to resist without this bit of insight, now...resistance would be impossible.

"It'll be okay, Becca."

She wished she believed that.

"Come on, I'll introduce you to everyone."

He did. Nick Saunders, the band's guitarist, and his wife Tracey. Alex Morgan, their new drummer. She knew Noah and Isabeau, of course, but spending the afternoon with them gave her new insight into their personalities.

Nick was the dedicated family man, Noah

the quiet leader. Dominic was the joker, and not surprisingly since they'd been best friends for years, one of the only ones who could pull Noah into a lengthy conversation. The youngest of them was Alex, who could only be described as a bit wild, a whole lot impulsive, and loud.

Then there was Isabeau. Although she appeared to be near the same age as Alex, she had a maturity that he lacked. She handled the large group, the noise and the upset, even the puppy piddling on her rug like she'd been made for the job. She kept up with the demand for food and drink while remaining an active part of the conversation.

A skill which Rebecca found impressive since she could barely stay afloat of the quickly changing topics.

Conversation rarely lagged and was often interspersed with teasing and laughter. No one was safe, everyone at the table being made the butt of a joke or well-meaning ribbing at one point or another, even herself. She found it all pretty amazing, really.

By the time they were done eating, she also found it all a bit overwhelming.

Which Dominic apparently noticed. Excusing them both, he stood, grabbed her hand, and pulled her out of her chair and toward the door below the staircase.

"Where are we going?"

He glanced back at her, his mouth slightly

curved. "You were wearing your shell-shocked look again. I thought you might like to see the studio."

"It's like the ER on a full moon."

He stopped at the top of the stairs, one hand holding the door open, the other holding her hand. Humor flashed in his eyes. "Are you calling us a bunch of crazies?" Bringing their joined hands to his chest drew her closer. "That's what they say about a full moon, yes? It brings out the crazies?"

She racked her brain trying to come up with a way to explain herself that wouldn't sound insulting, but couldn't come up with anything. He arched an eyebrow, and she shrugged. "Listen, I didn't mean...I mean, I guess that's what I said but..."

A flash of amusement crossed his face. "Becca, don't worry about it. We've been called worse, believe me." Releasing her hand he motioned for her to precede him.

"I honestly wasn't trying to be mean," she explained, leading him to the lower level. "For a relatively small group, you sure make a lot of noise. That's really all..." Her thoughts trailed away as she reached the bottom step. "Wow."

The room they stepped into was similar in shape and size to the first part of the great room above. It even shared the wall of windows and view of the foothills. But there is where the similarities ended.

The floors on this level were hickory, the walls and ceiling, even the couch and chairs, white. At the far end of the room was a wood and glass door leading to the backyard, but oddly enough, every other door in the room – and there were three of them – were commercial doors. White metal with glass centers and slow closing bars at the top. The view through the doors was obstructed by drawn shades. "This is your studio?"

"Part of it. This is the lounge area, where we do a lot of the writing." Dominic moved further into the room, and she followed, past a drum set and wall of guitars, some hanging and others on racks on the floor. He pulled open the only door on the left side of the room. "This is the gym."

The instruments called to her. Black, blue, electric, acoustic. There were so many of them. Some old and battle scarred, others more beautiful than she could have imagined. Her eyes didn't know where to land, there was so much to see.

She peeked into the open door and was startled to learn they had more than just a few weights and benches lying about, they literally had a gym. Not the type that school kids bounced basketballs in, the type most people paid an exorbitant amount of money to join. "No wonder you're so fit."

"Performing night after night for an hour and half a pop is more tasking than it looks." He closed the door and moved to one on the other side of the lounge.

Rebecca stuck her head in. "It's a closet?" With another door just across from it.

"Not exactly." She followed him into the space, really just a tiny closet void of anything other than paint. "Soundproof rooms technically don't exist," he explained. "All rooms, walls, ceilings, floors, let sound through; it just depends on the volume and frequency of the sound."

"So, the little closet?"

"Is actually an air-lock. It's all about airtight construction. Putting it simply, where air goes, sound goes." He opened the next door and they stepped into the studio.

Walls somewhere between gray and purple gave way to a soaring wood ceiling. A ceiling that wasn't flat, as you would expect, but a congregation of angles and shapes creating a pattern that reminded her of looking through a kaleidoscope. It was beautiful. Truly a work of art.

A second drum set sat on her left, with even more guitars in stands. On her right was a wall with, surprise, more doors and a large window. A microphone and music stand centered before the window.

"The first door is the isolation booth—"

"Which is used for what, exactly?"

"Mostly vocals. It's pretty much a smaller

version of the one you're standing in. The room with the window is the control room."

Curious, Rebecca peeked in the window. "What is all of that?"

Dominic shrugged. "A bunch of things, really. Mixing consoles, monitors, a multitrack recorder, digital audio workstation—"

Only getting about half of that, she held up her hand to stop the flow of words. "I only understand bits and pieces of that," she admitted, looking around. "Let me guess, the door at the end is another air-lock?"

"That's a closet actually." She gave him an *are you kidding me* look and he chuckled. "Honest. The one next to it is the air lock."

"So, if no room is actually sound proof and it's all about the flow of air, then wouldn't this ceiling be like a giant megaphone tunneling the sound to the floor above?"

When he didn't reply, she turned her attention away from the gorgeous ceiling and settled it on the gorgeous man smiling at her. "What? You're looking at me like I said something utterly ridiculous."

"No, I'm looking at you like you said something utterly charming."

"Whatever," she said, her cheeks warming.

"I'm serious. Are you actually interested in this or are you humoring me?"

"It's really very interesting."

He looked at her a moment before

responding. "The ceiling is all about acoustics."

"Balancing absorption and reflection to provide a favorable acoustical environment, got it."

Dominic blinked.

"What?"

He shook his head. "The flow of air is controlled via—"

"Air-locks."

"Yes. Also with sound isolating walls, ceilings and floors which affect the amount of sound able to travel through."

"Floors? How do you get sound isolating floors?"

"The one you're standing on is a floating floor with sand between the concrete pad and the flooring."

"No kidding?" She hadn't lied; it was all really very interesting. Oh, it made sense if she thought about it, but up until today she hadn't. She understood sound waves and the human ear. But directing or interrupting the flow of those waves, especially when related to his career was very, "Fascinating."

Rebecca walked back through the air-lock and into the lounge, where she tipped her head up and checked out the ceiling. It didn't look anything like the artfully crafted wood ceiling of the studio. Not that the room didn't have its own appeal. The photos and artwork, album covers and tour memorabilia that covered the walls were just as intriguing.

A framed and matted magazine article drew her attention and she crossed the room, discovering it was a biography of sorts—an outline of the band from their formative years through the tragic death of their drummer, Danny Treybourne, ten years ago and their subsequent break up.

Rebecca turned her head and met Dominic's gaze. She pointed at the article. "Is this for real? The part about you having never played a note before joining the band?"

He lifted a shoulder. "Yeah."

"That's incredible. How old were you? The first time you ever picked up a bass?"

"I don't remember."

"How do you not remember the first time you picked up a bass?" She certainly remembered the first time she saved a life. You didn't forget moments like that.

"I remember the first time I picked up a bass, Becca. Just not my exact age."

She stared at him, silently. Waiting for him to crack, to explain a statement she knew couldn't possibly be true. The first time he'd ever picked up a bass would have been life-changing. That wasn't something you forgot.

When he said nothing, she waited some more, finally breaking and calling him on his bluff. "Bullshit."

CHAPTER FIFTEEN

The last thing Dominic wanted to do was have this conversation with Rebecca. He never had this conversation. Not with interviewers, the other members of the band. Not with anyone. Talking about that time in his life would be equivalent to exposing a festering wound that never healed, then handing the person a knife to add another.

No. No way. Not going to happen.

He looked at her and had no idea what to say. No bleedin' clue how to get her off this topic and onto one that didn't require revisiting a place he tried very hard never to go. She didn't want to hear about his childhood. That he'd been raised by his grandmother, a sweet woman who on more than one occasion had gone without in order to provide for him. That he went commando, something she'd once confessed to finding sexy, not based on comfort, but because food had been of greater importance than underpants.

Dom didn't care to see the look of pity she would surely have if he admitted he'd been a loner, not by choice, but circumstance. Kids

196

didn't want to be friends with the poor kid, the one whose clothes were always a bit too big, a bit too small, or a bit too ratty. It was far more fun to make that kid the butt of jokes and ridicule.

"Dom," she said with terrifying gentleness.

Well shit, there it was. Compassion. She knew there was something behind his silence and had already softened to it. "Like I said, I don't remember."

The soft look vanished beneath a mask of frustration.

He let out a long, slow breath he hadn't realized he'd been holding.

She shifted away from the article, then wandered over to the wall of sales certificates, more commonly referred to as gold records. Hung in chronological order from their first album, *Awakening*, through *Ascension* and ending at *Immortal*. Three albums, three levels of success. The sales numbers and awards themselves didn't seem to hold her attention, which shifted to the album art and corresponding official group photo. At each photo she would stop, lean closer, then run her finger over his image.

And each time, he felt it like a physical touch.

Every.

Single.

Time.

She turned to the wall opposite and once again he found himself letting out a long breath. This wall was safer territory. Much safer.

"Those are Isabeau's." Her awards, platinum and double platinum discs, for each of her four albums.

"She told me she used to play, but I never made the connection." She tapped one of the awards. "I have this one."

He did his best to keep his voice neutral so she wouldn't pick up on his inner turmoil. "Most everything she owned was lost in a fire. Those were at her father's place along with her piano. She tried to lock them away in a closet when she moved here, but Noah wouldn't have any of it."

"Why would she want to lock these away?"

The same reason he didn't like talking about his past. "Bad memories, I suppose."

"Hmmm." She kept moving, circling the room, finally stopping in front of the collection of guitars. "Which is yours?"

There were a few of his there, but the one he preferred was, "On your left."

"This one? It's beautiful." She settled her hand on the headstock, trailed it over the tuning pegs and down the strings. She dipped the tips of her fingers into the cutaway not once, but twice before circling the neck and sliding back up.

Dominic shuddered, his mind conjuring images of her stroking something other than his bass.

"I thought basses only had four strings?"

He had to clear his throat to speak. "Traditionally yes, but you can get them with five, six, or more. It all depends on the range required, mode of playing, or just personal preference. That one is my favorite."

"Because of the number of strings or the instrument itself?"

"Both. The small string spacing makes it a bit difficult to slap, but the neck is incredibly fast, and the tones I can crank out of it are bloody spectacular."

She locked her gaze with his and gave him the ghost of a smile. Then slid her hand back down the neck, easing the tip of her finger between the strings and teasing the fretboard.

Christ. She was driving him crazy. He'd much rather experience her touch on his skin, the tips of her fingers slipping along the length of his erection.

There was only a few feet separating them and Dominic closed it. He covered her hand with his.

She rolled her eyes. "Are you one of *those* guys?"

"What guys?"

"The ones who get all over protective about their possessions. Especially their cars."

"It's not my car you're stroking, Rebecca." No, it was *him*. Literally and figuratively.

199

The instrument beneath their hands is what made him who he was. Saved him from poverty, a miserable childhood, and a lonely existence. Maybe not that exact instrument, but one like it. It woke him up to the skill he could have never imagined he had—a natural ability to create music and make people happy. It took him away. Made him forget.

It was an extension of himself. A part of him that no one, *no one*, was allowed to touch. Yet here she was. She'd picked up his guitar much like she'd picked him up. Without hesitation.

Dom stared at her, his heart pounding hard and fast in his chest as he was struck with the realization that she'd touched more than his bass. She'd touched a place deep inside him, filling a void he'd spent years pretending didn't exist.

She met his gaze and he became lost in her eyes. She was so damn beautiful. He scooped up a chunk of her hair where it lay like fire across her shoulder, then handed her the proverbial knife.

"I was thirteen."

She didn't ask what he was referring to. She didn't have to. "The first time you picked up a bass."

"Danny and Noah were fifteen." Liking the feel of her hair between his fingers, he scooped up more. "I think they felt sorry for me. I was a scrawny, sickly kid with the worst case of hero worship ever. Desperate for just a taste of what they had, I followed them everywhere."

She was trembling as she whispered, "What did they have that was so special?"

He opened his hand and watched the strands sift through his fingers. "Each other." Becca looked up at him, a war of emotions on her face. When she didn't ask any more questions about his childhood, he breathed a sigh of relief.

She took his hand in hers and lifted it to her mouth, pressing a kiss against callouses on the ends of his fingers, the pad of his thumb. Then she lowered it from her lips and repeated the action with her fingertips. "Did you know that you play in your sleep?"

"Play what?"

She laughed and it went a long way to clear the cobweb of memories from his mind. "The bass."

"Yeah?"

"You didn't know?" She turned so that her back was to his front, spooning while standing. "Every night you tap out a beat on my hip." She slipped her fingers between his and pressed against her stomach. Tipping her head back to look up at him, she used her own to thump his thumb in a stilted rhythm.

He took over for her, adjusting the beat to match the song they'd been working on all week.

"Mmmm, just like that," she hummed.

"Every night?" He buried his nose in her

hair, inhaling the incredible scent of her. It was surprisingly arousing holding her so intimately among the collections of his life.

"I have to assume so as you've never *not* done it when I've been with you."

"Interesting." But not nearly as interesting as the shift in her breathing.

"Dominic, when we were together before?"

Still tapping along to the tune in his head, he slid their joined hands down her stomach. He knew it was the right thing to do when her breathing hitched. "Yeah?"

"Who did you play with?"

"Besides you? No one."

She chuckled, then sucked in a breath as his hand slid even lower, the tips of his fingers dipping into the top of her jeans.

"I mean musically. Black Phoenix was..."

"Black Phoenix was what?" he whispered against her temple.

She gripped his wrist. "I'm trying to have a conversation and you're seducing me."

"So, it's working?" he asked, rocking his hips against her. Hers responded in kind before she stepped out of his arms with a groan. "I can't help it," he said, running his gaze the length of her. All the way to her toes and back up, stopping to admire the way her shirt hugged her pebbled nipples. "I can't control myself around you. You're the one who pressed yourself against me."

"I suppose I did, but I..." A glance at her chest had her cupping her hands over her breasts. *"Dominic!"*

"Becca."

"We aren't doing that. Not here where anyone can walk in on us."

"I'll lock the door." When that didn't appear to change her thinking, he hit her with the other. "You can scream all you want down here. It's soundproof."

A hint of color pinked her cheeks. "Nice try. You already told me soundproof rooms don't exist."

He stalked forward. "The same techniques that were used in the studio were used out here."

Her eyes flashed heat, hunger and desire and his dick swelled to attention.

She backed into the wall with a stuttered cry. Dom placed his hands on either side of her head and leaned in. "I was playing with a band called Blind Man's Alibi when I first met you. Noah was just talking about bringing Black Phoenix back together. We were brainstorming on a new drummer since Danny's death is what tore the band apart in the first place."

She stared up at him, eyes warm. "Blind Man's Alibi? What type of music was it?"

They were pelvis to pelvis, chest to chest, the hard points of her nipples pressed against his pecs, and she still wanted to talk music? He wanted to strip the clothes from her body and slide home. Right here, in the middle of place where his entire life was literally on display. "A bit harder rock than Black Phoenix. More growl."

"Interesting name."

He skimmed his mouth along her jaw. "I had nothing to do with the name."

Becca settled her hands on his hips, then slipped them beneath his shirt. "What's it like?"

He sucked in a breath as she traced his abs with her fingertips. "What?"

"Performing."

"Better than sex." He nuzzled beneath her ear and she moaned. "Okay, not *better*. It's thrilling. An incredible high that leaves you hornier than a three-peckered goat."

She choked out a laugh. "That's quite an image. And you, all you have to do to find relief is give a woman a look, talk to her in your low, sexy accent and her clothes come off."

"Who needed to talk?" he asked with a smile that quickly faded. "I figured out a long time ago that's not what I wanted. Women who knew nothing about me, who just wanted bragging rights. It leaves you feeling empty." He ran the back of his fingers down her cheek, dragged his thumb across her lips. "I'll never forget the first time I saw you."

"You sauntered over, all confidence and arrogance. 'The Stud'."

"I wasn't confident," he confessed as he pressed his lips against the pulse point in her neck, and was rewarded with a shudder. "I was completely gobsmacked for the first time in my life. You were so incredibly beautiful. Heart-shaped face and big green eyes—curvy, the way a woman should be." He slid one hand in her hair, the other down her hip. Her eyes darkened. "Then you looked up, totally unimpressed, unaffected while I stood there hard as a brick and struggling to form complete sentences." It didn't escape his notice that nothing much had changed.

"You failed miserably."

Dom could only chuckle at the shared memory.

"You spewed cheesy come on lines at me."

"Which you shot down by saying—"

"You don't actually think that line will work, do you, Stud?" She laughed.

"Totally unaffected," he repeated.

She slipped her hands out from beneath his shirt and he had to stop the moan of frustration from breaking free. Her voice dropped. "I was never unaffected."

"No?"

"No." She brushed her fingers down his cheek, her gaze locked on his mouth. "I could tell you expected me to be impressed, to know who you were. You expected me to be just like every other woman there."

205

"You're not like any other woman I've met." His brutal honesty surprised him. He wondered if it had the same effect on her.

"You don't think so?" Her voice came low and throaty, incredibly sexy. "What if I told you that the whole time you stood there stumbling," she leaned closer, until her lips brushed the shell of his ear as she whispered. "I stood there pinching my thighs together, pretending I wasn't close to coming at just the thought of you touching me."

"Jesus." At her confession he lost it. He pressed in close and kissed her. Hard. And just a little bit rough. She had her hands fisted in his hair, he had his filled with her ass. He couldn't get enough of her. He lifted his head as someone cleared their throat. *"What?"*

"I didn't mean to interrupt," Noah said drolly.

Becca's cheeks flamed bright red. She released her hold on his hair and pressed her face into the center of his chest. God, she was adorable. "So, why did you?"

"I thought you'd like to know I'm taking Isa to Lake Tahoe."

That brought Dom's head around to focus on Noah. Immediately, he noted the twinkle in Noah's eye, the smile that was more than just him catching them in a compromising position. "Yeah?"

"We'll be back in time for the photo shoot next week."

206

"Sure thing."

"Lock up when you leave."

"Always do."

Still grinning like a loon, Noah didn't move.

"Noah?"

"Yes?"

"We're kind of in the middle of something here."

Noah pointed at himself. "You wanted me to leave?"

"Yes."

"Hmmm...."

Becca started to shake. At first he wasn't certain what was going on. Then he heard the first giggle. She pressed her face harder against his chest, attempting to muffle the noise but it broke free.

Dominic chuffed out a breath. He had a hard-on the size of California intimately pressed against the woman of his dreams, who happened to find his situation laughable, all while his best friend looked on like it was just another Sunday afternoon. She was right, they were a bunch of crazies. "*Noah*. Was there something else?"

"No."

"Then sod off!"

Noah chuckled as he started up the steps.

Dom refocused on Becca, who was laughing even more hysterically now.

The footsteps halted. "FYI," Noah called

down. "Everyone else has left. And in case you were wondering, the couch there is very comfortable. I highly recommend it."

"Tosser," Dom muttered at the retreating footsteps.

The door clicked closed.

"What exactly is a tosser?" Becca voiced then squeaked as Dominic lifted her off the ground. "What are you doing?"

"You heard him, he recommends the couch." After dropping her on the piece of furniture, he pulled his shirt off over his head while simultaneously toeing off his shoes. He removed a condom from his back pocket and stuck it between his teeth as he undid the top button of his jeans. Then he stopped. "You're wearing too many clothes, Rebecca."

She dragged her eyes over his body, igniting a fire inside of him. "Sorry, I got distracted." She opened her mouth a little, then closed it. The sight of her pink tongue swiping across her bottom lip made his dick press against his fly.

"You don't happen to still have those leather pants, do you?"

He shook his head, tossed the condom on the cushion next to her. "What leather pants?"

"The ones in the photograph over there. Very sexy. If I'm going to have an affair with a rock star I think I should get to see those leather pants in the flesh at least once, don't you?"

He felt a little thrown. A feeling he was

starting to get used to around her. "You like those, huh?" Her eyes went glassy with arousal, telling him she liked those leather pants. A lot. His blood heated. "What if I told you I still have them? What exactly do you want to do with them?"

"Take them off you," she said breathlessly. "God, you are a beautiful man. I just want to lap you up."

"You can't use your imagination?" he asked, his voice thick and hoarse even to his own ears. "Pretend I'm wearing them now?"

"It's not really the same, is it?"

He swore viciously.

Becca smiled. Then she snagged a finger in his belt loop and pulled him closer. She trailed her free hand down his abs, stopping where the tip of his dick peeked out the top of his jeans. Eyes still on his, she leaned down and bathed the head with her tongue.

He couldn't hold back the low growl of pleasure even if he'd wanted to.

She unzipped his jeans, and eased them down his legs so he could step out of them, took his hard-on in her soft hand and kissed the tip a second time. "So beautiful," she whispered. Then she took him into the heat of her mouth.

He buried his fingers in her hair, half of him wanting to hold her there and thrust deeper, the other half wanting to pull her away. She dragged her fingernails up his inner thigh and cupped his balls, squeezing gently before releasing. With a hard suck of his flesh she withdrew, then licked up his length, circled him in a wet sweep, and traveled back down again, this time taking him to the very back of her throat.

"Rebecca," he groaned, struggling for control. "Don't stop. Please, don't stop." *Dear God, she's reduced me to begging.*

Her hands and lips devoured him, rendering him helpless. She commanded his undivided attention as she quickened the pace, swirling wetness over his head and adding her free hand to the mix. Every suck of her mouth was followed by a stroke of her hand and squeeze of his balls. Suck, stroke, squeeze. Faster and faster as she worked him closer and closer to the edge.

He fisted his hand in her hair and guided her head as she devoured him, relaxing her jaw and taking him deep. With his dick still touching the back of her throat she swallowed, working his balls to the contraction of her throat. He tried to hold back, to prolong the intense pleasure, but had virtually zero control when she touched him. His hips surged, as she swallowed again and then he was coming harder than he ever had before.

His breathing slowed and he gathered himself, muscles protesting every movement. His heart thudded in his chest, his dick jumped.

Stunned by what he'd just experienced, he looked down at Rebecca and blinked. She remained fully dressed, lips swollen, face flushed. Her hands were still on him, one at his hip, the other stroking the inside of his thigh, and somehow that alone was enough to bring him back from the dead.

"My God," she said. "Already?"

Pulling her to her feet he undid the fly of her jeans, pushing them and her panties to the floor in one sweep. The move back up her body took her shirt, which left her standing before him in nothing but a pale green bra. Simple enough to rid her of, only when he reached for her, she stepped to the side. "Becca?"

"You'll like this, trust me." She reached up, not to the back of her body, but between her breasts. With a flick of her fingers, her breasts sprang free, baring her to his gaze.

She was right, he liked it. A lot. Even more when she spun him around, centered her hand on his chest and shoved, dropping him onto the couch and effectively reversing their positions.

Then she was on him, climbing onto his lap so she straddled him. Fingers plowing into his hair, fisting the length. She pressed her mouth to his, tugging at his lower lip with her teeth, then sweeping her tongue inside when he moaned.

Shocked to discover he could taste himself in her mouth, he froze, then planted both hands on her back and pulled her closer, as his arousal shot into uncharted territory. She was like a fire that burned, yet left him desperate to feel the flame again. An addiction he feared he would never kick.

She wrapped her fingers around his erection, pulling a groan from deep inside of him. "God, Becca." He covered her hand with his, and stroked himself along with her, showing her how hard and fast he liked it. Then he slid his hand up her smooth thigh and dragged his thumb over her wet flesh. "You feel so good."

Her head fell back, mouth open, hair trailing down to brush his knees as a helpless whimper broke free. She couldn't hold still, her body moved over him, her back arched, calling to him with her open thighs, her scent. He answered the call, closing his mouth over a nipple as he pushed two fingers inside of her. Her muscles began to tremble. She rocked her hips, grinding against his hand.

He slid his other hand over her hip, down the cleft of her ass to tease her from the other side. She was so hot and wet, so close to the edge she groaned in pleasure. In a bold move, he lightly clamped his teeth down on her nipple, pushing her into orgasm. She came with a scream, convulsing around his fingers and damn near taking him with her.

"Dominic—"

"I'm here, beautiful."

"What did you do to me?"

He laughed, reaching out blindly for the condom he'd tossed on the couch. "If you have to ask, I must have done it right." He used his teeth to rip open the package, then rolled the condom on. As he gripped her hips he lifted her up. Her eyes were closed, head still thrown back. "Open your eyes, Becca, look at me."

She lifted her head and locked her gaze with his. A smile played across her lips as she took him in hand, and positioned him at her opening.

He let her down slowly, drawing out the pleasure as she sank onto him, taking him deep, deeper still. He didn't move, allowing her to adjust to his size, taking his cues from her as to when she was ready. He didn't have to wait long. One hand on the back of the couch, the other on his shoulder she rode him, her lush breasts against his chest, body pulling him in. His grip on her hips was tight, controlling her as she ground her clit against his stomach.

Through it all her gaze stayed on his, allowing him to see what he did to her. And then she was coming again, her body milking his, coaxing him to follow her over the edge.

Dominic groaned, then came with a whisper of her name in her ear. When he could stop trembling and blink his vision clear, he realized something had changed for him. He'd just given Becca more than pleasure. He'd given her everything he had.

213

CHAPTER SIXTEEN

"Tell me something," Karmen said, placing her cafeteria tray on the table and dropping into the seat across from Rebecca's. "Does he have that same just-had-the-most-amazing-sex-of-my-life look on his face or are you alone in this?"

Since she'd been sipping her coffee, Rebecca choked. "Who?"

"Well, that answers question number one." Karmen forked a bite of chocolate cake into her mouth. "That it really is a just-been-thoroughly-laid look on your face."

"I thought you said it was a just-had-the-most-amazing-sex-of-my-life look?"

She stopped with another bite of cake halfway to her mouth, then leaned forward, her voice dropped conspiratorially. "Was it? The most amazing sex of your life, I mean."

Rebecca looked at her friend, amused despite herself. She mirrored Karmen, leaning forward in her chair, elbows on the table and hand curled around her mug. "I'll never tell."

"So it was. *Nice!*" Her cell phone whistled. Karmen pulled it off her waist, glanced at it, and dropped it to the table with a frown.

"Problem?" Rebecca asked her.

"It's nothing. Just...let's get back to you, shall we?"

"Karmen?"

Her friend waved her off. "Do I even need to ask the identity of the man who put that look on your face? Tell me it was the walking fantasy."

"I'm sorry but you'll have to be more specific." She grinned broadly, enjoying teasing Karmen.

"Tall, Dark, and Studly."

"I don't know who—"

"Ha! Don't even pretend you don't know who I'm talking about. How can I live vicariously through you if you won't admit it was Dominic Price who rocked your socks off over the past three days, leaving you with that just-been-thoroughly...sorry, I've-just-had-the-best-sex-of-my-life look on your face!"

The room fell silent around them. Rebecca stared at Karmen, horrified.

"Oops. I said that rather loudly, didn't I?" Karmen asked, then grinned unrepentant.

"Fantastic. The rumor mill will now be abuzz with talk of me."

"Sweetie, tongues are already wagging about you." Karmen washed down the cake with a swallow of milk.

Chocolate milk. Chocolate cake and chocolate milk; her two comfort foods.

Before Rebecca could ask her if everything

215

was okay, Karmen continued. "Jeanine in X-ray? She's telling everyone how she saw you and a patient from a few weeks back, all over each other in the parking lot."

"No. We never..." They'd never done anything inappropriate on hospital grounds. "In the parking lot?"

She forked up another bite of cake. "Mmm-hmm. Something about a sexy number pulling up in a sexy number and giving you the hottest kiss she'd ever seen."

Shit. That may have actually happened. A flush of warmth spread through her at the memory.

"She describes it for anyone interested, and I have to say it does sound pretty hot." Karmen slid her a long look. "Did he really cup your jaw and hold you in place before moving in for the kill? Hold you there, and look at you for a while first? Because *da-ham!*"

A shadow fell over their table and Rebecca looked up to find Nathan, coffee in hand, the corners of his mouth pulled down in a frown. His gaze danced between her and Karmen before settling on her. "I was going to ask if you were aware of the stories spreading through the hospital like wildfire."

Fantastic. If they'd reached Nathan, they'd already burned out of control.

"But it's apparent you have."

Rebecca grimaced. "Don't ask me what I

216

think I'm doing."

"By the sound of it you know exactly what you're doing," he replied, his tone a tad too patronizing for her liking. Her mood just shy of pissed-off, she narrowed her eyes at him. Nathan sighed. "You're a grown woman, Rebecca. You're free to make your own choices."

"Yes. I am."

With that, Nathan walked away.

"Poor man," Karmen said, her gaze on his retreating back.

Rebecca finished off her coffee. "Nathan? Only the other day you called him a jerk."

Karmen shrugged. "He's still a jerk, just a broken-hearted one."

"He'll get over it."

"I'm not so sure, Bec. That was a pretty heavy look he gave you before walking off. Maybe you're the one who should be called 'The Stud.'"

Rebecca rolled her eyes and pushed to her feet. "I'm out. I have some charts to finish before the end of my shift. Thanks for helping me feed the gossip mill."

Karmen flashed a smile. "Anytime, girlfriend."

She was smiling as she walked out of the cafeteria heading for the emergency department, smiling as she passed a couple of young volunteers, heads tipped together in conversation, smiling when she felt the hand circle her arm.

And then she was pulled around, slamming against a hard chest. "Mr. Masters—" She tried not to panic, to regulate her breathing and calm her heart rate. They were in a hospital, surrounded by people. He couldn't hurt her here. Why would he try?

But there was no denying the hatred in his eyes as he glared at her, or the force with which he squeezed her arm.

"I know what you did, letting my son die like that."

"Letting him die?" Rebecca straightened, shifting her shoulder in a way meant to encourage him to release her arm. His grip tightened to the point of pain. "Mr. Masters, I didn't let your son die. I fought like hell to save him. But his injuries were too severe."

"It wasn't my fault. I'm a good father...It wasn't my fault."

She set a hand against his shoulder, felt the raggedness of his breaths move through his body. "No one is saying it's your fault, Mr. Masters."

He stepped closer, the scent of whiskey wafting off him. "You need to be stopped." Eyes narrowed into slits, he glared. "You shouldn't be treating patients."

Rebecca's heart skipped a beat as she scanned the hallway for help. Dread crawled over her skin when she found none. *Where the hell was everyone?*

Cold fingers circled her other arm, digging in, demanding her attention. He pulled her closer yet, in an embrace that mimicked intimacy, and bile crawled up the back of her throat. "You shouldn't be treating patients," he repeated, mouth so close to hers his breath brushed across her lips. "Someone needs to stop you."

****

Rebecca had just finished reporting the incident to hospital security when Nathan walked up. He flicked his glance over her, checking for injuries, then then shook his head. "I just heard what happened."

"I'm okay," she said, straightening her lab coat, folding and re-folding her stethoscope before shoving it into her pocket. "He didn't hurt me."

"Thank God." He settled a hand on her arm, blinking with surprise when she jerked away. "Rebecca?"

"I'm sorry." The adrenaline in her system manifested itself in a severe case of the jitters. Her body trembled, her fingers fidgeted, and her skin felt hypersensitive. It was all a perfectly normal part of the winding-down process, but that knowledge didn't make dealing with it any easier. "That's how...I'm sorry."

He was looking into her eyes. Whatever he

saw there must have reassured him because he nodded. "What did security have to say?"

"That they'll keep their eyes open. Notify all shifts to be watchful in case he returns." Which he wouldn't. He was nothing more than a grieving father looking to place blame on someone other than himself. "But that I should remain alert."

"Good advice. You should probably also make sure you don't arrive or leave alone until they figure out what the guy wants. Why don't you grab your things and I'll take you home?"

The glass doors swooshed open and Dominic stepped into the ER. At the sight of him, Rebecca's heart tripped along at a stuttered beat. Her breath backed up in her throat. "I've got that covered."

Dominic's piercing blue eyes settled on her. A smile spread slowly across his face and her chest expanded to the point she feared it would burst. She did the only thing she could do. She walked right into his arms.

They closed around her warm and taut with muscle, held her tightly as she absorbed his warmth and strength. "You're trembling."

"Because she was attacked," Nathan said matter-of-factly.

"I wasn't attacked," she was quick to correct as the body against hers went still.

"What else would you call it, Rebecca?" he asked angrily. "You were attacked and

220

threatened."

"Christ, Becca!" Dom pulled back, cupping her nape to look into her eyes. "Someone threatened you?"

"No. He didn't threaten me." Not really. He only said she needed to be stopped, not that he planned to stop her. "Nathan is overreacting." She hadn't thought it was possible, but at the mention of Nathan, Dom's body tightened even more. She smoothed her hands over his back, communicating with touch that there was nothing for him to worry about.

His gaze lifted, focusing on a spot behind her. "Ah, the infamous Nathan."

"Dr. Nathan Connelly. I don't believe we've had the pleasure," Nathan said not at all welcomely.

"Who said it was a pleasure?" Dominic returned.

Rebecca stepped back in shock, her gaze bouncing between the two of them. They were sizing each other up, and she knew neither could miss their differences. It was like looking at polar opposites. At least physically. As far as similarities went, they both had a streak of arrogance running through them, a confidence that could grate on the nerves. Were both above average in looks, and at the moment, they were also both puffed up like peacocks, squared off in some sort of male posturing as old as time.

Silence reigned. Finally, Nathan broke it.

"So, this is your Englishman?"

"Bloody hell," Dominic muttered.

"Charming," Nathan replied.

Rebecca shook her head. Having had enough of their nonsense, she stepped away.

Only to have Dom snake his arm around her waist and pull her back. "Becca, tell me it isn't him."

"What isn't me?"

"Dominic—"

"Are you shitting me?" He looked Nathan up then down, an expression on his face of a bad taste in his mouth. *"Him?"*

The confident smile drained from Nathan's face. "What's wrong with me?"

Dominic continued, his attention focused solely on her. "A fucking vibrator is better than this guy."

Nathan's body went taut, hands clenched at his sides. "Fuck you!"

Gazing back at him, she gave Dom the truth. "Aside from the arrogance, he was about as far opposite from you as I could get."

"Fuck you, too, Rebecca."

She felt more than saw Nathan walk away. She would deal with him later. Right now her only concern was the man standing at her side, arm slung around her waist, looking more than a little uncomfortable over what he'd just learned. She considered him carefully. "You don't have to be jealous, you know."

"I'm not jealous."

His reply came far too quickly for her to believe. "Dom."

"I'm not jealous, Becca."

If that was true, what was the emotion swimming in his eyes? "It was only one night."

"Fuck," he muttered beneath his breath, then released her and stacked his hands atop his head. He looked around the emergency department, gaze never settling in one place for long. He looked everywhere but at her. "Is there anything you need to finish up or are you ready to go?"

"I need to hang up my lab coat and get my purse from my locker."

"Sure. I'll wait here."

True to his word, she returned to find him standing in the exact spot she'd left him. Deep in thought he seemed completely oblivious to the people around him, a few of them staring openly as if they recognized his fame. It was either that, or he just didn't care.

As she approached, he pushed away from the wall he'd been leaning against and slipped an arm around her waist. Uncustomary quiet settled over them. By the time they reached the car, Rebecca couldn't take it any longer.

"Hey," she said, snagging his hand as he pressed the remote door release. "Talk to me."

He cupped the side of her face, brushed his fingers over her temple; his thumb over her jaw,

223

her lips. He replaced his thumb with his mouth, delivering a soft caress of lips, a slow seduction that promised so much more and had her reaching for him.

But he had already stepped back, and was holding the car door open as he waited for her to slide in. He closed the door behind her, then he circled the vehicle, slid behind the wheel, and drove her home in silence.

CHAPTER SEVENTEEN

If Dominic had thought learning Rebecca had slept with another during their time apart was like a punch in the stomach, meeting that person face-to-face had been a kick in the dick.

He sat in the middle of Rebecca's living room while nursing an ale. The lights were dimmed. Muted sounds of running water carried to him from the other room, and he knew she was standing beneath the shower, running hands over luscious curves. She'd invited him to join her, yet here he sat, imagining what her body looked like all soaped up and wet instead of seeing it for himself.

He'd turned her down. Not because he didn't want her with a violence that twisted his gut. He did. But because he knew he couldn't touch her right know without wondering if the noises she made while he pleasured her, were the same she'd made for the doctor.

And didn't that just make him a sorry sonofabitch?

Nathan.

Dr. Nathan Connelly.

She couldn't just pick a man with golden boy

good looks; he had to be a doctor? A fucking trauma surgeon to boot!

Dr. Nathan Connelly, chief trauma surgeon at her hospital and an arrogant prick.

He knew, because as Becca went to fetch her purse, he'd pulled his mobile from his pocket and checked the man out.

Bloody wanker.

Lifting the ale to his lips, he took a pull, admitting to himself that he was bothered more by the guy's appearance than his arrogance. Arrogance he understood, but...that was the type of guy Becca was attracted to? The type of guy she wanted?

Polished.

Put together.

Creased dress slacks.

Proper shoes.

Every close-cropped hair in place, and hands that looked as if he got regular manicures.

Respectable.

Fuck.

If this was the type of guy Becca wanted, he didn't stand a chance in hell. What was it she'd said to him? *"Aside from the arrogance, he was about as far opposite from you as I could get."* Who knew she could throw a punch without ever making a fist?

Sinking farther into the chair, Dominic tossed an arm over his eyes with a sigh.

A door opened, the sound of Becca moving

about the bedroom reached out and grabbed him by the throat. He told his legs to get up and go to her, but they wouldn't cooperate. Not with doubt still gnawing at him, with fear weighing him down.

He could argue with himself all night, telling himself that she was with *him*, not the doctor. Reminding himself that she'd claimed to have only spent one night with her surgeon. But that wasn't the full story. There was more to it than she was letting on. More that she didn't want him knowing. He'd stood in her kitchen and listened to her end of the phone conversation with her mother and he knew. The man Rebecca's family expected her to have been with was Nathan.

Looking around her condo Dom had to wonder who could blame them. She was educated and smart, with more degrees hanging on her wall than he had gold records. Just the title of the book sitting near his elbow had made his eyes cross. Why the hell would they want someone like him for their daughter? He wasn't well-dressed or polished or anything like that.

He was a long-haired, ear-ringed bass player with a foul mouth. A forty-year-old man with no family and no home to speak of who lived out of a suitcase. A man utterly besotted with a woman completely out of his league.

And clueless what to do about it.

She'd allowed him back into her world, now

what? How did he move what they had from 'fun' to something more? How did he let her know he was serious about them becoming serious?

Would she even care? Or would spilling his guts, sharing his secrets with her cause her to leave him? Like that damn little voice inside, the one he could never silence, told him would happen.

Surging up, Dominic slammed his ale onto the side table with enough force it foamed, spewing out of the top like a volcano. Running down the sides of the bottle and dousing her book. "Fuck!" He snatched up the book, then sat there like an idiot, holding it in the air as it dripped. He had no napkins, no towel.

He had no breath left in his lungs.

Rebecca stood in the doorway between bedroom and living room, hair knotted atop her head. Wearing a black lacy corset, that pulled her waist in and pushed her breasts up to spill over the top, and black stilettos on her feet, she was the picture of sex. Garters hung from the bottom, but she wore no stockings so that when she started across the room, hips rolling provocatively, the garters slapped against her thighs.

Every nerve ending in his body went on high alert. For a long silent moment he couldn't speak. Not a damn word came to mind.

She came to a stop in front of him, removed

the sopping book from his slack fingers and tossed it to the floor. A hand to his chest pushed him back into the seat, then with a press of the remote next to his ale bottle, the room was flooded in music. She started to dance, hips rolling and swaying in time, the garters slapping her ass.

His music he realized just before his brain went soft.

The rest of him went rock hard.

Dominic leaned back in the chair and actually began to sweat. He shifted to give his painfully hard erection a bit more room. Sweet Jesus, she was incredible. He already knew the ways she could move her body while it was joined with his, but to watch her do so in time to his music was intoxicating.

He'd seen women dance before many times, but none quite like Becca. She managed to incorporate modern dance moves with classic rock and sprinkle in the art of strip tease.

Mesmerized, he could only stare as she moved her hand down the front of her body to cup herself. A move so sensual and exciting he had to readjust his position in his seat. She turned her back to him and rotated her hips again so her garters bounced, and his grip tightened on the arms of the chair.

The tempo of the music increased and so did her movements. Twirling around she flipped her head in a way that caused her hair to slide free of its topknot while she arced her hips in a circle.

He groaned aloud.

The corset went first, revealing a bra that cupped her round breasts but left her dark pink nipples free for his eyes to devour, and a barely there pair of panties.

He began to shake.

The first crack in his resistance appeared as she placed her right foot on the left arm of the chair and locked gazes with him, while she took her right hand on a tour down the front of her body. Between bare breasts that begged for his mouth, over her navel to slip into the front of her panties. Her eyes closed, head tipped back, and he could only watch in wonder – dick straining, palms itching – and imagine just what her fingers were doing. He locked his gaze on her hand, wet his lips, and then she was moving again, trailing her damp fingers up her body.

The expression in her emerald eyes told him she knew she had him exactly where she wanted him as she slipped her visibly wet fingers between her lips and sucked.

"Becca," he managed before his vocal cords froze.

She'd turned, and ass poised directly before him, began to work those tiny panties down her legs. Giving him an eye level view of her hidden treasures.

Dom was out of the chair like a shot. He had to have her. Hard. Fast. *Now.*

Afraid that if he didn't get inside her within the next few moments he was going to spontaneously combust, he swept her into his arms and made it to her bedroom in record time. He dropped her on the bed on her hands and knees. "Don't move," he threatened, voice raw.

She flipped all of her hair to one side and looked over her shoulder as he struggled to work his zipper over his straining cock. A provocative smile played along her lips. "I wouldn't dream of it."

Unzipping, he pushed the denim down his thighs, and ripped open a condom, fumbling with the damn thing he was shaking so hard. A second attempt wasn't any more successful when she scooted to the end of the bed, dropped her feet to the ground, and fisted her hands in the bedspread. "Hurry, I want you inside me."

Out of his mind with need, he finally managed to slip a condom on before he grabbed her hips, held her in place and buried himself inside of her in one hard thrust. He wasn't slow, and he wasn't gentle. He'd lost gentle a while back along with reason. He thrust harder and harder, their loins slapping together as he fisted a hand in her hair.

A small, wild sound vibrated up her throat as her body clenched hard. He bent over her back, sinking his teeth into her shoulder, pumping steadily, not slowing even as she whimpered his name. "Dominic, don't stop. Please don't stop loving me."

Driven by his own urgency, he fisted his hand tighter, urging her head to the side so he could look into her eyes. He trailed his fingers over her hip, slipping between her thighs and lightly pinched the bundle of nerves at the apex of her sex. She moaned, shuddering in his arms.

He held her there, right on the edge, as he whispered *"Mine."* Her body bucked hard, struggling against his hold. "You're mine, Rebecca."

"Yes," she cried out, her body arching and shaking. Releasing the comforter, she reached behind her, grabbed his ass and pulled him deeper. Then he was thrusting hard, groaning, his entire body contracting with her as they orgasmed together.

****

"Welcome back."

Rebecca came awake slowly, stretching muscles taxed by their lovemaking. Dominic was on his back in the center of her bed, arm up, palm cushioning his head. She was pressed against his side, wrapped around him like he was her personal body pillow. "Mmm, how long was I out?"

"A while."

Stacking her hands on his chest, she dropped

232

her chin atop them and smiled down at him. "Did you sleep?"

"No."

"Uh-oh."

"What?"

"You have a very serious look on your face. What are you thinking about? Climate change? The current state of the economy?" A very satisfied smile curved her lips. "The earth-shattering orgasm you so recently gave me?"

"You," he replied softly, brushing her hair off her cheek. "Us."

A thrill moved through her knowing he was thinking about them as an 'us'. She kissed his sternum, his pec, then licked his nipple.

He slid a hand into her hair. "Becca."

"Are you going to pull my hair again," she whispered against his chest. "Because that was hot."

"I'm going to paddle your ass if you don't behave."

Would she enjoy being paddled by him? Her entire body quivered. He groaned in response. Feeling feisty, Rebecca bit his pec, laughing when he rolled her beneath him in self-defense.

"How come I've never met your parents?"

Her laughter vanished as if it had never been, sucked away by the shock of his words. She stiffened, turned her face away from him. "They're not important."

He cupped her face and made her look at

him. "They're your parents, Becca."

"What about you?" She pushed against his chest, chuffing in frustration when she couldn't budge him.

"What about me?"

She didn't want to talk about her parents. Her father's disapproval. Her mother's willingness to give up her career for a man who didn't appreciate her. "It's not like you ever talk about your family."

"I talk about my family all the time. I even took you to brunch with them."

She shook her head. "Those are your friends."

"They're so much more than that."

"Dom—"

"You want to talk, I'll tell you anything you want to know." He rolled off her, shifting to a seated position. "I don't talk about parents because I don't have any, Becca. I'm an orphan. At least I think I am. Who the hell knows for sure?"

How could he not know whether or not he was an orphan? "What is that supposed to mean?"

"My mum was an addict who sold herself for drugs. My father...who knows? She probably didn't even know who he was. It's a bloody miracle I'm alive today; that she didn't stumble into an alley for an abortion. She sure as hell didn't want me," he said matter-of-factly.

Jesus. As an addict, it was a miracle she'd carried him to full term.

"Lucky for me, I had a grandmother who came looking the moment she learned of me. Found me, half-starved and filthy next to mum's body."

"Your mother died in childbirth?"

"Nah, she OD'd afterward," he said casually, looking like it was no big deal, even perfectly normal, but it wasn't. "Took one look at me and shot up so much heroine she—"

"God, Dominic."

"I spent a few days in hospital before gram could take me home."

She knew what he wasn't telling her. It wasn't just malnourishment that had put him in the hospital. He would have been born addicted to his mother's drug of choice. Rebecca looked up at her beautiful man, and an ache went through her. Pain for what he suffered, even if it was at a time he never would recall. She linked her fingers with his and squeezed his hand.

Dominic sighed. "Gram did her best for me. Raised me until I was sixteen."

She knew his answer before she gave voice to the question. "Why only sixteen?"

"She died." The anguished whisper had her crawling closer. Kneeling at his side and wrapping her arms around his trembling body. "The day after my sixteenth birthday."

"At least you had Noah and the band." He'd

had Noah. When the only relative he had in the world passed, Dominic had Noah and the band. They'd become his family, just as he'd said. "Oh my God," she whispered. That first day, the very first day after they'd met, he'd taken her to meet Noah, and she hadn't even..."Why?"

"Why what?"

"You introduced me to Noah." He'd introduced her to his *family*, an action that was usually reserved for those special people you wanted to build a relationship with. "But you walked away from me. Why?"

Dominic shrugged, his eyes shuttered.

"No, no you don't. You said you'd tell me anything, Dom, so tell me why?"

He murmured something too soft to catch and then shook off her arms, shifting to the edge of the bed. "You were going to leave me."

"No, I wasn't."

"You would have. Eventually."

She stared at the hard planes of his back, his broad shoulders, tight with tension, and thought about what he said. How she was going to leave him. Even though she'd never planned to. She'd fallen in love with him, why...

Everything clicked into place. He'd been let down over and over again in life. "Even Noah let you down."

"Noah's never let me down."

"Yes. When he left music. He walked away from it, from you. He left you, just like your

236

mother, your grandmother."

"He was grieving over Danny's death. He was lost."

Her thoughts were in a whirl, which made sense since the earth was shifting beneath her feet. "Yes he was, but that didn't make the hurt less, did it?"

Dominic pushed his fingers through his hair and stared at the ceiling. He didn't deny it.

"Dom?"

"I didn't want you to look at me one day and wonder what you'd gotten yourself into. I know what I am, Becca. I'm a long-haired, ear-ringed, uneducated musician. I come from trash and only excel at two things; playing the bass and pleasing a woman." His voice was a conflicting mix of pain and pride.

"Dom—"

"What if you looked at me one day and decided anything was better than another minute with me?"

"What?" she whispered. Her chest ached. "Jesus, nearly three years lost because—"

"I'm not a good guy, Rebecca. My entire life I've used women then tossed them aside as if they were nothing. Just like my mum tossed me."

Just as he'd tossed her. Those words went unspoken, but they hung in the air between them.

"But I've changed. It's taken me forty years

237

to be the man I am today. I'm still not perfect, but I..." Surging to his feet, he scooped his jeans off the floor and pulled them on.

"What are you doing? You're running again?"

"Is that what you think?"

"You're getting dressed."

Sadness filtered into his expression. "And your mind automatically goes to me running? I thought we were past that."

"You're getting dressed," she argued. "Forgive me if I'm having flashbacks of the last time you crawled out of my bed in the middle of a confession." She watched as he pulled his shirt on over his head, stuffed his feet in his shoes. "You're getting dressed," she said a second time, heart in her throat.

"I need to be alone."

"Why?" He didn't answer and she panicked. He was leaving her, running away. Again. She'd thought this time would be different. This time *had* to be different. "I'm sorry," she whispered. He cared for her. He hadn't said the words but the truth was in his actions. The way he looked at her, touched her. How he kept coming back no matter how hard she pushed him away. He wasn't the same man he'd been before. So why was he leaving? "I'm sorry about what I said about everyone letting you down. Just...don't go."

He cupped her chin. "It's not what you said, Becca. It's what you haven't said."

238

"What I haven't said?" Did he want her to relive the moment, the most painful moment of her life? The moment where she confessed her love for him and he ran? She loved him. She loved him so damn much it hurt. But the fear that her confession would be the final push out the door for him was too ingrained to shake loose. She wouldn't relive that moment. She wouldn't.

A storm rolled across his eyes. "You've got nothing, huh?"

"Dominic, I—"

"I pour my heart out to you, share with you the whole ugly truth about my life, and you still haven't shared one thing about your family."

Her family? Why would he want to know about her judgmental, managing parents?

"Do they know about me? About us?"

She looked away.

He dropped his hand from her face. "So, we're all in the dark about each other. That's telling, isn't it?" He stared at her, then stared at his feet. "I know I'm not good enough for you, Becca. I've always known it. I just..." His voice broke. "*Fuck!*" He walked out the bedroom door.

"Wait! Dominic!" She tried to follow him, only to become tangled in the sheet. Struggling, she pulled the sheet off the bed and took it with her. Just as the front door slammed. "Dominic!"

She was too late.

He was already gone.

CHAPTER EIGHTEEN

The next morning Rebecca stood outside the door to Dominic's apartment, waiting for him to come to the door. His car was parked in its usual spot at the base of the stairs, but so far her knock had gone unanswered.

As had all the calls and texts she'd sent.

She was starting to become worried.

Raising her fisted hand, she rapped once in the center of the door before it was pulled open, revealing Dominic in all his glory. Shirtless, shoeless, he looked more than a little rumpled and sleep deprived.

And gorgeous.

With a bite mark on his pec.

She was surprised by the rush her mark on his flesh gave her. *Mine. You are mine.*

She had to clear her throat to speak. "I tried to call you."

"I wasn't ready to talk to you."

Ouch. "Can I come in?"

He didn't move.

"Or not," she mumbled. "Look, I'm sorry."

"For what?"

She laughed uneasily. "Not going to make

this easy on me, are you?"

He arched his eyebrow. He stood leaning against the doorjamb, one ankle balanced over the other, hands tucked into his front pockets. His eyes, usually so vibrant, were flat and wary.

"For being afraid. For not trusting you. I know how different you are, I..."

He didn't say a word, just watched her as she floundered.

Damn, she'd hurt him more than she'd thought.

"You say you only excel at two things, but being a woman I feel the need to tell you they're both pretty spectacular talents."

No change, not even a smirk.

"I'm sorry, Dominic, mostly for hurting you. I didn't mean to hurt you." She swallowed past the lump in her throat. "The things you said yesterday—you're right, but you're also so very wrong."

"That's clear as mud."

"I know, but I can't really explain it to you. You'll have to see it for yourself. Will you come for a drive with me?"

His brow furrowed. "Does it require a suit, because I don't have one?"

Rebecca glanced down at herself and sighed: perfect hair, perfect clothes. Perfect—for her father. "You know what, you're right." She slipped out of her jacket while still on the landing outside his apartment. Then began unbuttoning her blouse.

A few catcalls rent the air, and Dominic's eyes flashed emotion for the first time that morning. Grabbing her by the arm, he pulled her into the apartment.

Where she began to pace and strip. "What the hell am I doing?"

"You're asking me?"

Wearing nothing but her bra and panties, she started for his bedroom. "I left a pair of jeans here the other night, didn't I?" She turned to find him still at the door, watching her. But at least his ubiquitous grin was back. Sort of. Spotting her jeans over the back of a chair, she shimmied into them, then looked down at her chest. "Can I borrow a shirt?" She crossed to his closet and pulled it open. The scent of him washed over her and for a moment all she could do was stand there and absorb. Then she reached in, pulled out a tee and slipped it on, checking out her reflection in the mirrored closet door. Not bad. The shoes, unfortunately, would have to stay.

Heading back into the living room, she discovered he still hadn't moved.

"Did you sleep at all last night, Becca?"

"No, why?"

He grinned. "The Energizer bunny wants his battery back."

"Very funny. Are you ready?"

"I don't think I am."

For a moment she felt off balance, as if he'd said one thing but meant another. "Too late."

"It is," he muttered. Only the grin on his face kept her from panicking at his words.

"Dom, you should probably finish dressing."

"You're wearing my shirt."

"So, put a different shirt on." Why did it matter what shirt he wore? He had a closet full of them, couldn't he just pick out another one? Men. She didn't understand them sometimes.

"I'd planned to wear that shirt."

"Fine." With a sigh, she pulled his shirt off and tossed it at his head. Oh, how she wished she'd managed to sleep last night. Even just a few uninterrupted hours would have helped. Without sleep she talked non-stop, saying the first thing that popped into her head without filter. The very last thing she needed to happen when facing her father.

She gave an unladylike snort. Like what she had to say would matter to her father. He hadn't approved of anything she did. Ever. But this was going to be the topper. The final straw that was going to push her father over the edge. She shook her head. She was mixing metaphors. Another black mark on her character.

She reached into the closet and pulled out a tee at random, not paying any attention past the softness of the fabric and pale blue color. Then she headed back to find Dom wearing both the shirt and his shoes. He was also wearing a very large grin.

She'd been played. She grinned back at him, unable to stop herself. "Just remember, you asked for this."

****

For the second time that day Rebecca stood outside a door waiting for it to open. Only this time her stomach was knotted with dread over what awaited her on the other side.

Her father was a difficult man. He was arrogant, opinionated and at times cruel. He had a set of standards that he considered desirable in a person and anyone who didn't fit them was unacceptable.

Not important.

Not worthy.

Shit. She exhaled a shaky breath as her hands began to shake. Dad was going to reinforce the fear Dom had of not being good enough and that terrified her. Chilled her to the bone. Dominic was everything and more than she wanted. She'd longed for his return for nearly three years. Now that they were here, about to face her father's disdain she had to wonder; would he still want to stick with her after seeing what loomed beyond the door?

"Hey." Standing at her right, Dom settled a hand at the small of her back and rubbed a little circle. "It can't really be that bad, can it?"

She looked into his eyes, and gave a stiff

smile. "Just remember, you asked for this."

"Shit. That's the second time you've said that to me this hour. Now you're making *me* nervous." He ran his gaze over her, stopping on her breasts. His eyes darkened. "I've changed my mind about this shirt. I don't want this one. Quick, trade shirts with me."

"Very funny. You don't have to tease me about my multiple changes this morning. I know I'm being ridiculous."

Dominic palmed her ass. He leaned over and pressed his lips to her ear. "You can remove your clothes around me anytime you want, Becca. Hell, I'll help you."

Rebecca choked out a laugh. The front door swung open. Her father's frown greeted her. "Hello, Dad. Can we come in?"

"Of course you can, dear," her mother said from just inside the house. "Richard, move back and allow your daughter and her friend entrance."

They stepped inside as her father closed the door with a snap. Rebecca didn't know where to start, so she went with the basics. "Mom, Dad, I would like you to meet Dominic. Dom, these are my parents, Richard and Camille."

"It's a pleasure to meet you, Dominic," her mother said, flashing him a genuine smile.

Her father…well, he didn't exactly growl.

"Very nice to meet you, Mrs. Dahlman."

"What a fantastic accent. Are you English?"

"Yes ma'am."

Which, because of his fantastic accent, came out sounding more like mum. Her mother went all dreamy eyed. Rebecca knew that feeling. Tucking her hair behind her ear, she stared at him for a moment, marveling. He was all relaxed charm, while she was a bundle of nervous energy. She shifted in her pumps and he settled a hand at the small of her back again. His heat soaked through the tee. She concentrated on his touch, and her pulse slowed.

"How long have you known my daughter?"

"Going on three years now."

"Really?" her mother said, pinning Rebecca in place with a look. "I wonder why she's never mentioned you?"

Dominic focused on Rebecca, too. She waited for him to spin a yarn about their relationship, or lack thereof over the past few years. At the very least she expected him to look to her to answer.

He surprised her by telling the truth. "Probably because I was a bleedin' fool and caused her pain when I should have been confessing my feelings for her."

Heart lodged in her throat Rebecca could only stare at him as she fought a desperate desire to ask what those feelings were.

Her mother's face registered surprise. "Oh, that's so sweet. Isn't that sweet, Richard?"

"Sure, sweet," he said, his tone indicating he

thought it was anything but.

"Oh, poo," she replied, waving him off. "Tell me, dear, what do you do for a living?"

Dear? Jesus, was there a woman alive he couldn't charm? Not that he had to work at it. He succeeded just by being himself.

As if he read her thoughts, Dominic winked at her. Then he focused all of his attention on her mother. "I'm a musician."

"Really? What type of music? Classical? Ooh, jazz perhaps?"

"Rock and roll."

Her father's look of disgust was impossible to miss. *Here we go.* Her stomach knotted.

Her mother chatted on, appearing to be genuinely interested. "Really? What instrument do you play? Are you famous? Would say, my neighbor's son know you?"

"Bass. And he might. We were very popular about ten years ago."

Camille smiled up at him, then stepped close. She cupped Dom's face as she might someone she'd known a long time, not someone she'd just met. "You have incredible bone structure. Truly wonderful genetics." She dropped her hand to his bicep and squeezed.

Good Lord, my mother is feeling him up!

"With your olive skin tone, I bet you're of Italian descent."

"I honestly don't know."

She studied Dominic a moment, an odd look

on her face. "He'd make beautiful children, Rebecca."

"Oh, my God," Rebecca mumbled, her cheeks burning.

"Look at you, all embarrassed. Your man here isn't embarrassed, are you dear?"

"Not at all," Dom replied with a grin.

"Like she hasn't already thought about what your children would look like," her mother whispered conspiratorially. "Do come with me, Dominic. I could use your help in the kitchen."

Stunned beyond words, Rebecca could only watch as they walked away.

"Menopause," her father stated dryly. "It's making your mother a little nutty."

****

Dominic sat at the kitchen table while Camille made them tea. She was an interesting woman, Rebecca's mother. Tall, curvaceous, with auburn hair a few shades richer than Becca's and eyes the same emerald green. She wore black slacks and a green silk blouse, hair pulled off her shoulders in a fancy sweep, and a pair of heels on her feet. At ten o'clock in the morning. If this was normal daily attire for the house, it was no wonder Becca had been at his door in a fancy suit.

Camille placed a cup of tea on the table before him, then eased into the chair opposite. She fiddled with the handle of her own cup, fingers sliding up and down multiple times before she took hold and lifted it to her lips. She eyed him over the rim. "You don't know your heritage?"

Out of all the things Dominic expected her to say, that was not one of them. "No ma'am. I don't know who my father was. Not sure my mum did, either."

She nodded, then worried her lower lip with her teeth. "Richard is all about breeding." She placed her cup back on the table and shrugged. "He's a Dahlman, after all."

Was he supposed to know what that meant? "I'm sorry?"

"His is a family of doctors, every one of them. Mother, father, grandparents, even his aunts and uncles. Cold people, really. Superior intelligence, which makes them top in their field, but lacking compassion." She shook her head. "Richard was the black sheep. Oh, he followed in their footsteps and went to medical school. Specialized, and became the best in his field. He didn't marry well."

"I would have to disagree with you there."

"Oh, you're a charmer, aren't you? No, I was a schoolteacher when I met Richard. A totally unacceptable career choice to a family of surgeons. However, he ignored his parents' warnings and married me anyway. It helped I was pregnant with Rebecca at the time." She smiled wistfully. "Rebecca is so much like her father."

Becca didn't sound anything like her father.

"She is smart, driven, stubborn. On the contrary, she has a softness he's never had. A compassion for people, young or old, rich or poor. And she's a dreamer."

"Becca?" He saw Becca as focused, always in control – unless he was pleasuring her – with her head firmly planted in reality. "A dreamer?"

"Oh, yes. When she was thirteen she dreamt of seeing the world. She wanted to be...oh, what is his name...Indiana Jones."

Becca?

"She put posters all over the walls of her room, papered every surface with her favorite rock stars, teen idols and faraway places she longed to travel."

No way. He smiled at the knowledge this was something he could give her: the rock stars *and* world travel.

Camille frowned into her tea. "Her father made her take it all down. Told her to get her head out of the clouds and forbade her to listen to that—"

"Rot?" he suggested, thinking it was a suitable word the stodgy, unfriendly man he'd met a few minutes ago would use.

"Close enough."

Her father sounded like a controlling ass.

"I should have put my foot down. There were so many things I should have stopped. She was already so different from everyone else, so much smarter." She fiddled with the handle of the cup again. "She needed normalcy. He gave her home schooling on top of her private education. Schedules and order. He's molded her since birth with one goal in mind: for her to become the next best neurosurgeon."

"Like her father," Dominic guessed. He wasn't sure how he felt about the idea of Rebecca as a neurosurgeon. She had the brains, but did she possess the desire? She'd never mentioned it, not three years ago or now.

Camille sighed. "There's a part of him that knows he pushes too hard, asks too much of her. He's not completely devoid of compassion. He loves her, but he can't seem to stop himself. Upbringing you know, years of receiving the same sort of treatment from his own parents. It's the only way he knows how to be."

Dom understood that, how upbringing and experience could mold a person. How difficult it was to go against something that had been ingrained in you from a young age.

"Her father pushes, and Rebecca takes it. I don't even think she wanted to become a doctor."

"Really?" How could that be? She'd always been so in tune with her job. So very good at it.

"Her one act of rebellion was her refusal to specialize in neuroscience."

Dominic blinked, doing his best to take it all

251

in.

Camille covered his hand with her own. "And you," she said softly.

"Me?"

"Richard won't approve of you. Rebecca knows that."

Because he was a musician, who'd crawled his way out of the shit.

Her eyes sparkled. "Yet...here you are."

His throat constricted. "You don't have the same concerns about me?"

Her smile took ten years off her face. "Breeding doesn't mean shit to me. My daughter does. And you, Dominic, are exactly what she needs. I could see it on her the moment she walked in."

"What?" he asked, hating the unsteadiness of his voice.

"Joy."

CHAPTER NINETEEN

"I spoke with Nathan yesterday," Rebecca's father said the moment her mother and Dominic stepped out of the entryway. "He says he's concerned about you."

"I'm fine, Dad. The man is harmless." Nothing more than a grieving father venting his anger on the easiest target. Her.

"That man is anything but harmless, Rebecca. Just look at your mother. She's already fallen under his spell." He shook his head. "And what he's done to you...it's disgraceful."

It took a moment for her to figure out who her father was talking about. "Dominic? What has he done to me, Dad?"

He took in her clothes, his frown deepening as he focused on her T-shirt. "It is impossible to mistake that scandalous shirt as belonging to anyone but him."

Scandalous? Her gaze settled on the shirt in question. She read the words plastered across her chest and barked out a laugh. *Bass players do it deeper.* How had she not noticed that? Rebecca laughed until her eyes watered.

Her father glared at her. "You have social

standing in this town, Rebecca."

"No, that would be you. I'm just an ER doc."

"Rebecca Jane—"

"What, Dad," she asked, hugging herself. It was always the same thing with him. It never changed. "I'm never going to be enough for you, am I? Not good enough, smart enough, successful enough. I'm a disappointment."

"Don't be ridiculous."

Hope blossomed, only to be crushed by his standard mantra.

"You just need to further your education. A mind like yours shouldn't be allowed to atrophy."

Disappointment nearly choked her. No worries. She'd been letting him down for years. "What about what I need?"

He gave her a look that suggested she couldn't possibly know what was best for her. "I want what's best for you, Rebecca."

"How is molding me into the mirror image of you what's best for me?"

"It's better than..."

"What?" she asked forcefully. "It's better than what, Dad?"

"That man."

She let out a breath and considered him. The person she'd spent her whole life trying to please. The one she'd bowed and bent to, altering her path and giving up what she wanted for. She wouldn't do it this time. Not anymore. Rebecca couldn't control the fine tremor of emotion that wracked her body. "*That man* has a name."

True to his personality, her father ignored her, his tone implying that a musician was the absolute worst thing in life a person could be. "That man is not for you. He's a musician, for God's sake."

"Yes, and a damn successful one."

"Rock music, how...disreputable."

"Richard," her mother warned.

Her father snapped his mouth shut.

Rebecca turned. Dominic stood next to her mother near the kitchen door. He'd heard everything. She pinched the bridge of her nose and said the first thing to pop into her head. "Fuck."

Her father's back went ramrod straight. "Rebecca Jane Dahlman, watch your language!"

"I'm not a child anymore, Dad."

"No, but you are in my house."

"You're right. For that I apologize." She dropped her hand away from her face and focused on the woman across the room. "I'm going to go now, Mom."

A frown marred her mother's face. "Come back soon, Rebecca. Bring Dominic with you."

There was a smile on Dominic's face. Not the one that always made her want to remove her clothes, but one that affected her just as powerfully. He grounded her, calmed the storm of anger raging inside. He'd heard everything. The insults and intolerance. Everything. Dominic knew that even though her father didn't know him, he didn't *want* to know him. Based on something as asinine as breeding and career. Still he smiled.

A smile that said he was there for her. A smile that said so much.

Her heartbeat settled just looking at him. Any doubts she had about bringing him here today fled in that one moment. They were in this together.

"You know what, Dad? Do you know what I see when I look at Dominic? I see exactly what I need. I need more than droll conversation and proper standing in the community. More than just a respectable career. In fact, I'm going to quit my job." *God, it felt good to say that out loud.*

"It's about time you went back to further—"

She kept her gaze on Dominic, as his was the only opinion that mattered. "I think I'm going to become a professional groupie."

His smile grew, shifting, changing. There it was, the one that made her want to remove her clothes. Desire curled low in her belly.

"I'll get a piece of shit blue Chevy that smells like cheese and follow the band from city to city."

"That's right," Dom said softly. "It was a Chevy."

Heat shimmered in the air between them at the shared memory. Was there time to take him back to her condo before her shift at the hospital? Or pull to the side of the road and take him in the backseat like the good old days? God, the rush of power and passion he brought out in her was heady.

"Don't do that, dear," her mother said softly. "I'm sure he'd let you on the bus."

Rebecca nearly choked on her tongue. By the sound her father made, he *had* choked.

"Camille!"

"Well, he would," her mother replied, unfazed.

"I would," Dominic agreed with a glance at her mother.

Rebecca shook her head and softly uttered, "Bloody hell."

****

Rebecca leaned against the car, with her face tipped toward the sun, and sighed. After the whole tour bus bit, she hadn't gotten out of the house fast enough. "Do you know how miserable I was as a child?"

"Yes."

She laughed without humor. "Thirty minutes with them and you've already figured that out?"

He brushed his fingers over her arm and Rebecca took hold of his hand. "The other day in the studio, you said you remembered the first

257

time we met. How you were...?"

"Gobsmacked. You were so beautiful. I couldn't believe that you wanted me."

She opened her eyes and locked onto his. "I don't understand that. I was never the pretty girl in school, Dom. I was the geeky little brainiac. The orange-haired, freckle-faced girl who threw off the curve and was ruthlessly picked on by the other kids."

He shifted her hand to his chest, directly over his heart, and flattened it beneath his. "I still like your freckles."

She ran her nails over his goatee as her heart skipped a beat. "I didn't fit in, so I buried myself in books. I was fifteen when I headed to college." And those years were worse than the others. "Far too young to be accepted. My father was so proud of me and I was so lonely and miserable. He expected me to follow in his footsteps, but I didn't want it."

Dominic squeezed her hand. She lowered her voice and told him the rest. "I'm not sure I ever wanted to be a doctor. It kept me separate, even as an adult. I was one of the 'elite'. Maybe at first I enjoyed it, kind of an 'in your face' to those kids who so ruthlessly picked on me. But all I've ever really wanted was to fit in. I just wanted to be normal."

"What the hell is normal, Becca?"

She closed her eyes and sighed. "I don't know. I've never known."

"Are you really thinking about ending your career?"

"Yes."

"What will you do?"

She opened her eyes and smiled up at him, losing herself for a moment in his blue depths. "You don't think I should become a groupie?"

"I think you should do whatever makes you happy."

"What if I don't know what that is?" She slipped her hand out from beneath his, running it over his pec, his shoulder, to brush her fingers over the red suture line from his accident. "I honestly don't know. I want to do more. I want to affect change in a person. Positive change. It seems as if all I see is the bad. I don't get to follow up, to see if any good comes from what I do."

"You save people's lives, Rebecca."

"Sometimes." And sometimes there was nothing she could do. They died no matter how hard she worked, or returned to the spouse who was abusing them, only to wind up back in front of her, beaten half to death. She couldn't take it anymore. She needed more positivity, more life affirming goodness. Her hand unconsciously tightened on his bicep. She closed her eyes, opened them. Blinked back the tears.

He pulled her closer, pressed his cheek against her temple. "You can't save everyone."

Her breath hitched as the remembered

image of the boy's broken body returned. "He was just a baby," she whispered. "Barely three years old."

"Ah, damn Becca, I'm sorry."

And his father. So angry, full of blame. A tremor went through her body.

"You can talk to me, you know."

"I know," she eased her head away so she could look into his eyes, while cupping his face in her hands. "And I will, I'll tell you just...not now. Not after Dad." She took a moment to pull herself back under control. "I'm not ashamed of you, Dominic. It's just that Dad...no one's good enough in his eyes and I...didn't want you to have to hear that. That's why I never brought you over to meet them."

"You were protecting me." A look came over his face that she couldn't identify. "You've done it again. You've left me gobsmacked." He wrapped his arms around her and pulled her closer. "You were trying to protect me," he whispered.

It took a moment for her sleep deprived brain to figure it out. Then she knew. Why he couldn't seem to string enough words together. Why he looked so astounded. She thought of his mother, the one person who should have protected him right from birth and how she had left him exposed and endangered.

"I guess I was." She caught the hot glint in his eyes and reached for him just as his mouth came down on hers. He wrapped her in his embrace, pulled her flush against his body and kissed her. In her parents' driveway. Where everyone could see. Rebecca threw her head back and laughed, too happy to contain it. Then she kissed him again.

This one took a little longer to recover from.

Dominic opened the car door for her. "Come on, I'll buy you an ice cream before you have to be at work."

"I'm dieting."

"Again with the dieting," he said as he slid behind the wheel. He put the key in the ignition, started the car and buckled up, all before turning to look at her. His gaze moved slowly over her. "Your body is perfect just the way it is." His voice was all low and completely sexy. Rebecca shivered. "But if you're that worried about it, you don't need to be. I'll burn the extra calories off of you when you're done with your shift."

****

"Oh. My. God. Girlfriend, how is it you didn't just melt into a puddle?"

"Who says I didn't?"

Karmen grinned and Rebecca knew if she were to look in the mirror, she would find the same grin on her face. One she'd been wearing all shift. Dominic did that to her, made her smile.

He made her happy.

He'd told her she needed to do whatever made her happy and she planned to. Right after her shift was over. She planned to recreate their first time and take him in the back seat of the car. God, she hoped he brought the convertible.

Then when he was still drunk on pleasure, she was going to tell him just how much he meant to her.

"Holy hotness, Batman."

She had no idea.

"Rebecca, you need to see this."

Pulled out of her thoughts by Karmen's shocked tone, Rebecca turned her head. And promptly swallowed her tongue. Holy hotness, indeed.

Eyes locked on his destination, Dominic strolled through the emergency department, oozing testosterone with every step. The lean, rangy body was encased in black, from head to toe. Black leather pants rode low on his hips, looking as if they'd been custom made just for him. Hell, they probably had. The leather hugged his thighs, cupped his sex, and shot her pulse into orbit.

On the upper half of his body he wore a button-front shirt, also appearing to be custom. Inky black, it reflected just enough light as he moved to showcase his broad shoulders, flat stomach, and muscular arms. A burst of heat snapped along her nerves.

Everything female in her stood up and took notice.

"Check out the roses," Karmen said in awe.

"What?" Clutched in his hand were red roses. Lots of red roses. So many she wondered how she hadn't seen them until now. Then she looked back at the man.

Gorgeous.

Rock star gorgeous.

And all hers.

"I hate you right now, you know that right?" Karmen whispered.

Rebecca laughed out loud. She couldn't remember ever being this happy. She was in love and it was a glorious thing. Oh, she'd loved him for years, but that was before she'd seen him go out of his way to calm a friend's fears, or the gentle way he held a child. Before she knew of his past; a past that could have destroyed him and instead molded and shaped him into the amazing, warmhearted man before her. The love she felt for him today was deeper, stronger and more powerful, and she couldn't wait another minute to tell him.

"Dom," she said softly and took a step in his direction as a sharp crack echoed off the walls.

Dominic smiled, then paled. His body jerked. His face lost all expression. The flowers fell to the floor.

A woman screamed. Karmen? She couldn't tell, her ears were ringing. People scattered.

Someone bumped into her with enough force she wobbled.

Dom sank to his knees amongst the roses, spread before him like an offering.

Rebecca pushed away from the nurse's station, stepping closer as another shot rang out.

Another scream, this one hers. Then a voice filled with hatred sounded. "Someone has to stop you."

The barrel of a pistol pressed against her temple; the metal hot enough to burn flesh. The acrid scent of sulfur stung her nose. Rebecca whimpered. She had to help him. Dominic. The man she loved with all her heart and soul. He was laying on the cold floor now, blood pooling around his body. "If you're going to do it, do it. Shoot me. Otherwise, let me help him."

"No. You need to know how it feels."

Dom wasn't moving. Neither was anyone else for that matter. People hid behind anything they could find, crouching on the floor with their arms protectively covering their heads. A quick glance assured her that Karmen was safe, having scrambled behind the nurse's station. Knowing that allowed her to return her focus to Dominic. Was he breathing? She couldn't tell. "I do. I know how it feels."

"No, you don't!" he snarled, his voice full of anger and pain. "But you will."

"Don't move!" An armed security guard

hollered as he burst onto the scene. "Release Doctor Dahlman."

Masters paid the guard no attention. "You don't know how it feels, but you will."

"Mr. Masters, drop the gun!" A second guard called out, as he, too, joined the fray.

The pool around Dominic grew. Frozen with fear, no one made a move to help him. Not one person. *The hell with this!* She took a step in his direction.

"Don't!" Masters growled with a snap of his wrist that smacked the pistol against her temple with enough force to wring a cry of alarm from her. His voice dripped venom. "I've seen you with him. You'll know how it feels soon enough. To watch helplessly as someone you love dies."

He was losing blood at an alarming rate. His life, spilling out, enveloping the roses. She needed to slow his bleeding or this madman's wish would come to pass.

Her mind only on Dominic, Rebecca dropped to her knees, going boneless to slip away from her attacker's embrace.

A shot rang out.

She closed her eyes, bracing for the impact of the bullet, then continued to crawl when the pain didn't come. "Dominic!" She moved her hands over him, searching for the bullet's point of entry. His skin was cool to the touch. Spilled blood soaked the knees of her scrubs, its

265

metallic scent driving away any lingering odor from the pistol firing. There, there was the wound. Frantic to staunch the flow, she removed her lab coat and pressed it against his abdomen.

His eyes snapped open, then slid back closed.

"Don't you dare leave me. Not like this. " She leaned over him, applying more pressure to the wound. "I love you. Do you hear me? I love you, Dominic."

Suddenly, Nathan was at her side, pushing her hands out of the way, trying to take Dominic away from her. "Rebecca, get out of here. Let me do my job."

She could barely see past the tears spilling from her eyes. Her hands were shaking, her breath coming in pants. "I can help you."

"No, you can't. You're too emotional." He began barking out orders—the same orders she should have been calling out. "Get out of my way, Rebecca!"

When she didn't move quickly enough, he gave the order to have her removed.

CHAPTER TWENTY

Rebecca sat in the doctor's lounge, her eyes dry, gaze aimed at the floor. She was alone but for the ticking of the clock on the wall. She didn't want to be alone. She'd changed into a clean pair of scrubs, washed Dom's blood from her hands, but she could still smell it. Still feel the warm wetness as it saturated her lab coat.

As if her thought had conjured them, someone walked through the door. A pair of Doc Martens appeared in front of her, marked with a stain of blood. She closed her eyes, knowing whose blood it was as well as the identity of her visitor.

"Bec," Karmen said softly, then handed her a bag with Dominic's belongings.

Rebecca dumped the contents onto her lap: a wallet, cell phone, and keys. "Clothes?"

"They're destroyed. I didn't think you needed them just now."

She didn't. She really didn't. She didn't need ever see them again. His clothes or the roses he'd been carrying. The roses that last she'd seen them had been soaked with blood. Her stomach lurched, breathing hitched.

"Rebecca?"

She knew that tone. It was the same one she used when delivering news to someone who didn't want to hear it. Bolstering her courage, she looked up.

And noticed something else in Karmen's hand. A small black jeweler's box.

"Bec, he also had this in his pocket."

Shock clenched her hard in the gut. Her hands were shaking so badly, she had difficulty taking the box from Karmen. Her breath came shorter, faster as pain washed over her. It couldn't be. Heart lodged securely in her throat, she opened the box.

And started to cry.

Huge gulping sobs that wracked her body, making it near impossible to remain on the chair. It was too much, it was just too much, and once the tears started, she couldn't control them. "Dominic," she whispered. "Oh, God, Dominic."

Karmen sat next to her, pulling her close, holding her against her chest, her arms wrapped tightly around her. Offering gentle words of comfort that Rebecca didn't understand. "It's okay sweetheart, he's going to be okay. He's in the hands of the best trauma surgeon in the state right now. Dominic's going to be okay."

He was going to be okay. He had to be. There was no other outcome acceptable because clutched in the palm of her hand, nestled in a black velvet jeweler's box, was an emerald and diamond engagement ring.

"He's going to be okay," Karmen repeated.

Once she was able to breathe again, Rebecca closed the box. She swiped the tears off her cheeks and picked up his phone. With a deep breath to steady herself, she pressed a few buttons, and waited for the call to connect.

She didn't have to wait long. "Isabeau, it's Rebecca."

****

People began arriving right away. Nick and Tracey, Alex and some girl, was it Karen? Rebecca got the impression even he wasn't too certain. A man named Joe Campbell, a Bobby...something. Too worried about Dominic, her brain couldn't hold onto the names. There were just too many of them.

When she received word that Dominic was out of surgery and in the surgical intensive care unit, they all moved upstairs where their numbers continued to grow until they filled all the chairs in the waiting area. All but two. The two reserved for Noah and Isabeau.

Having been in Tahoe, it took them longer to arrive. Knowing that after their race to get to the hospital the first place they would go was straight to Dominic, she had paved the way for them, letting the staff know they were his family.

The room abuzz behind her, Rebecca stood at the window looking out into the hallway. She watched the doors leading to S.I.C.U and chewed on her thumb. Isabeau came out first. Pale, blinking back tears, hand over her mouth she leaned against the wall. Then she straightened and walked into the waiting area.

"Isabeau, I'm—" her words were abruptly cut short when the other woman walked straight to her and wrapped her in an embrace. She held her, no accusations, no anger, just comfort.

Rebecca started to cry.

"He's going to be okay," Isabeau assured her.

Rebecca should have been the one offering reassurances, after all she was the doctor. She'd spoken with Nathan, read Dom's chart, seen with her own eyes his vitals were good. He'd been shot in the abdomen resulting in a ruptured spleen with peritonitis. He was going to need lots of blood transfusions, but he was going to pull through.

"He's tough," Isabeau continued.

"He's going to be fine."

"Good," she sighed. "Good."

"I'm sorry."

"What for?"

Rebecca pulled away. "It's my fault. The shooting, it's all my—"

"Stop it!" Isabeau ordered, taking her by the shoulders and looking into her face. "You can't take responsibility for someone else's actions. Especially someone who is unstable. Trust me; this is something I know a thing or two about."

"I knew the man was angry, that he blamed me for the death of his son. I should have told Dom to stay away." Her stomach clenched. "I honestly never imagined this would happen."

"I know you didn't, how could you? Listen to me, Rebecca, if you had told him, you would have had a shadow. Instead of staying away, he would have spent every shift at your side."

Rebecca grinned, imagining the gossip that would create.

"What happened to the man?"

"Hospital security was forced to shoot him, but he'll live." Rebecca took a moment to study the tiny woman in front of her. "You're remarkably calm."

"I know." Something in her tone said she was as surprised by it as Rebecca. "Dominic is strong and he's got you. He'll pull through. Right?"

"Yes." She'd make sure he did.

"Good because Noah," Isabeau faced the door and waited. A few seconds later Noah stepped out, his face drawn and pale. "Noah needs to hear that. Excuse me."

Isabeau walked out of the waiting room and straight into her husband's arms, who held onto

271

her like she was the only thing keeping him vertical. Hands fisted in the back of her shirt, he pressed his face to the top of her head.

Rebecca looked away, allowing them a moment of privacy.

****

"Jesus, Bec, we're going to have to call security and get someone up here. Word of the party you're having will spread through this place like wildfire and things are going to get hairy."

Sprawled in the chair, head propped on her hand, eyes closed, Rebecca only grunted. She knew what Karmen was looking at—a room filled to bursting with musicians. Singers, drummers, guitarists, they filled every available space. Sharing stories about Dominic, cracking jokes. Singing.

That's the part that startled her the most. The singing. Luggage had been carried in with a few of them and someone had broken out a guitar. Next thing she knew, there were three guitars being played and two people singing. Not for attention, as some might think, no, because music was something they all had in common and it appeared to calm them.

"Holy shit," Karmen exclaimed, having another fan moment. She'd been having a lot of those. "That's Joe Campbell!"

"I know, I was introduced."

272

"Joe Campbell, Rebecca, from Blind Man's Alibi."

Rebecca nodded and opened her eyes. "Dominic performed with them once."

"Sweetie, you really need to broaden your music knowledge. Your fiancée—"

She shivered at the word.

"—*discovered* Joe Campbell and introduced him to Black Phoenix's record label. The rest is metal history."

Rebecca looked to where Alex and Joe sat shoulder to shoulder, talking quietly. Joe started playing his guitar and Alex nodded, joining him by slapping his hands on his knees like he was playing his drums. "How do you know this stuff?"

"I follow their music. Blind Man's Alibi has three albums, two of them platinum. That man right there is the epitome of Rock God—rich, uber-talented, and fucking hawt."

The rock god stood, stepped away from the noise, bringing him closer to where Rebecca and Karmen sat. He fished his phone out of his pocket and punched a number into it. Then he looked at them and flashed a crooked smile while waiting for whoever he'd dialed to pick up.

Karmen grabbed Rebecca's knee and squeezed.

"Easy girlfriend," Rebecca whispered with a chuckle. But even she got a little flutter when that deep, heavily accented voice took on a tone that bespoke intimacy.

"Hey, Sunshine…that is, if I have the right number. I had to use a bloody mirror as the wankers wouldn't read it to me. Why do you have a computer greeting as your mobile message? I was hoping to hear your voice." Tucking the phone back into his pocket, he smiled again before dropping back into his seat. This time when he picked up the guitar he started to sing. With more growl than Noah used, just as Dominic said. Someone handed their guitar to Noah, who soon joined in.

Karmen squeezed again. "Have I mentioned how happy I am that you're my best friend? I can't believe this is going to be your life. You're going to invite me over all the time, right?"

Rebecca laughed, happy to have her there to lighten the stress.

"We should probably call security." Someone new entered the room, drawing Rebecca's gaze. Karmen looked too, then mumbled, "Holy shit, never mind."

He was a large man, tall, broad and built with a capital B.

Joe stopped singing and greeted him. "Hey man, glad you made it."

"I hit the road the moment I heard from you. There's someone else claims to be looking for this group." He motioned over his shoulder as another man stepped in. This one just as large.

The first had brown hair trimmed military short and the most beautiful mocha skin Rebecca had ever seen. The second was bald with a blond Fu Manchu mustache and arms covered in tattoos.

"Dad." Isabeau stood, making her way over the sprawled legs and empty guitar cases to the bald one, who immediately wrapped her in his tattooed arms and pulled her against the broader of the two chests.

"Dad?" Karmen whispered.

"You're okay?" Isabeau's father asked after he released her.

Isabeau nodded. "Yes."

"How about my grandchild?"

Isabeau settled her hand on her lower abdomen in the way mothers instinctively did. A move that spoke of love and protection all in one motion. "Perfectly healthy."

"You're expecting?" Rebecca asked.

"You're pregnant?" Joe said at the same time. Then stood and slapped Noah on the back. "Congratulations!"

Noah moved to stand at his wife's side. Where he was immediately pulled into a brief hug from Isabeau's father.

"Thomas," Noah said, ending the embrace in that pat on the back men tended to share. "Your doppelganger there is Gary, friend and bodyguard to Joe here." He pointed to Joe who was still next to Isa.

Thomas nodded. "Joe and I met at your wedding."

Rebecca stood as Isabeau motioned to her. "This is Rebecca Dahlman, Dominic's fiancée."

"How?" Rebecca startled. How did she know? She'd been in Tahoe for days and Dom hadn't even asked yet.

"The rock is hard to miss," she replied with gentle smile.

"So, he finally pulled his head out of his ass, did he?" Thomas asked in a tone that had Rebecca's spine snapping straight. Then he flashed a charming smile and wrapped her in a bear hug. "He'll pull through," he said softly, his words indicating the depth of his feelings.

"Yes," she muttered against his chest. Discovering a comfort she never expected in this stranger's arms, she returned his embrace then stood there for a moment soaking up his strength. It felt like a father's hug should. Something she hadn't ever gotten from hers.

"Wait," Noah said. "Joe, how did you beat Gary here? You're supposed to be in what, Ohio, touring?"

"Uhhh..."

Isabeau nodded.

"I was already in California when I got your message. Here for the birthday party your wife is throwing you, mate."

Isabeau shrugged in response to the look on Noah's face. "Early birthday party as it's the only way I could keep you in the dark about it."

"So the photo shoot we have scheduled later this week?"

"Is actually your party," Isabeau confirmed.

"Dr. Dahlman?" The room went silent as all eyes turned to the newest arrival—a nurse from the surgical intensive care unit. "He's awake and asking for you."

CHAPTER TWENTY-ONE

It was the pain that first assured Dominic he was alive. Clawing at him, sinking its teeth in and wrenching him from sleep. He looked around the room, at the machines hanging on the wall near his head, beeping softly, the LED screens so bright they hurt his eyes, and discovered he was alone.

"Rebecca?" he managed to croak. What the hell? It felt like someone had set fire to the back of his throat. "Rebecca," he said again because she was all he wanted.

Still no answer.

Shifting on the bed sent a wave of nausea over him. He broke out into a sweat. An alarm sounded.

Someone pushed through the door.

Finally.

"Becca?"

The hand that touched him was cold. The breast dropped within inches of his face as the alarm was silenced, too small. She didn't smell right.

Not Rebecca.

He closed his eyes against the pain.

278

"Mr. Price, my name is Alice. You're in the surgical intensive care unit after being shot. Do you remember getting shot?"

Of course he remembered it. He'd been in the ER, looking at the most beautiful woman in the world, wondering how she would react to his proposal when a crushing force hit him, taking him to his knees. He'd tried to stagger to his feet, but his legs wouldn't work.

Jesus! Struck with panic, Dominic tested his legs. Severe pain shot across his lower back, but thankfully they moved.

"Mr. Price, are you in a lot of pain?" Her voice sounded matter-of-fact, like it didn't matter to her one way or the other.

What kind of question was that? Of course he was in pain. No one found themselves in hospital to take tea.

"I'll alert your surgeon. He can—"

"That's not the doctor I want to see."

Alice smiled down at him. "I understand she's in the waiting room with quite a few of your friends. I'll make sure she knows you're awake."

Dominic closed his eyes and must have drifted off, for he awoke to warm hands. One stroking the hair away from his face, and the other resting atop his left hand. "Rebecca," he whispered, then opened his eyes to her beautiful smile.

"For an orphan, you sure do have a lot of family."

He grinned weakly. At least he tried to. "Who's all here?"

"Alex and his girlfriend."

"Tammy?"

"I'm pretty sure he called her Karen."

"Figures," he mumbled.

"Nick and Tracey. Thomas—"

"Isabeau's dad, really?" Surprising. "He's…"

"Intimidating, I know."

"Huge," she corrected. "And…sort of sexy."

Dom's eyebrow went up.

"There are a few more—musicians from what I gather. Joe Campbell, your manager, and of course, Noah and Isabeau, who you failed to tell me are expecting." She sighed. "They're a noisy group. Thankfully the waiting room is pretty isolated."

"They can be," he admitted. It hurt to talk, but there was no way he would tell her that. So he lay on the bed, holding her hand, thumb smoothing back and forth over his ring. On her finger. God, he was a lucky bastard. Not just because he had survived.

"Every time I look up, there's another one walking in. There's nowhere left for anyone to sit down, but it doesn't stop them. They've been entertaining me with stories about you."

He could only imagine the stories they were sharing about him. "Bloody wonderful."

"They are," she agreed and he smiled even though that's not what he meant. "They all love you so much."

Even though it hurt, he raised her hand, brushed his lips across her knuckles. The ring, she still hadn't mentioned. But, damn, it looked good on her finger.

"Is your life always like this?"

"I can't say as I've ever been shot before, so no." He looked closer, at the dark bruising that circled her eyes. "You're totally knackered, Rebecca. That motoring mouth of yours is probably the only thing keeping you awake. Why don't you lie down? I'll shift over so you have room."

She touched him. She kept doing that, touching him, his arm, his face. Not that he was going to complain. Hell no. Her touch was calmly reassuring. "There's nothing I would love more than to crawl in that bed with you, Dominic. But there are time limits to visits in intensive care. Any minute someone will be coming in and shooing me out the door."

He tightened his hold on her hand. "You just got here."

"And already you can't keep your eyes open. You're in pain. Admit it."

"I'm fine."

"Dominic," she warned.

"Don't go, Rebecca. Just...stay with me."

"I'll only be as far as the waiting room. I'm not going to leave you." She leaned forward, touched her forehead to his. "I'll stay right here as long as they'll allow me to." The hand that cupped the side of his face trembled. Her voice dropped an octave, cracked as she whispered. "God, I thought I'd lost you." There were tears in her eyes. She blinked and one fell to his cheek.

"Becca." Dominic slid his eyes closed again and swallowed past the lump in his throat. For a while there, he thought she'd lose him, too.

"Every time I close my eyes I see you there. Bleeding. Dying."

"I didn't die, Becca."

She sighed then her hand was on him again, swiping her tear off his cheek. "There's something you need to know." She didn't wait for his response, just kept talking. "All of the people waiting on you, your friends and family? They all think we're engaged."

"Do they?"

She looked down to where he continued to hold her left hand, his thumb moving back and forth over her fingers, toying with the emerald he'd had in his pocket as he walked into the hospital...how long ago was that now?

"I didn't want to lose it." She smiled and his breath left him. "Jesus, Dom, could it be more ostentatious?"

"You don't like it?"

282

"I love it," she admitted reverently.

He raised her hand into his field of vision and smiled. "I stood in that store and suddenly knew exactly what had possessed Noah. I knew why he wanted bold capital letters."

"Why is that?"

"It sends the perfect message. You see, I'm a bit enamored with you," he admitted.

She swallowed then brushed her mouth across his.

He took a moment to catch his breath. "I guess this means you're not opposed to marrying a disreputable rock and roller?"

"I'll let you in on a little secret. I love my disreputable rock and roller. His ridiculous music and his earring, his too long hair." She brushed her hand over his hair, pushed it out of his eyes. "That long-legged, arrogant, too-hot-to-handle stud with the heart of gold? That's who I fell in love with."

"Too-hot...Jesus." He closed his eyes, opened them. "That man you speak of?"

"Yes?"

"He didn't come from much." Even though he was in pain, he wanted to make sure she knew of his origin, understood what she was saying yes to.

"I don't care where you came from, what's important is who you are. If I didn't already know just what kind of man that was, that room full of people would tell me."

"Rebecca."

She touched him again and his eyes drifted closed. "I've tendered my resignation. How do you feel about starting a family?"

His breath hitched, his body tightened. Bad move, as it set off an ache across his lower back. And an alarm on the monitor. "Afraid I would disappoint right now."

She reached over him to silence the alarm. "Stop it," she said, the order softened by the smile on her face.

"Lost too much blood to get it up."

"You could probably do it. You'd just pass out when all the blood left your head for—"

"My other head?"

A laugh burst out of her. "Yes."

"Let's wait then. I'd like to say I was conscious during my child's conception." His mind was spinning, and not just from the thought of procreating with her.

"Probably a good idea. Besides, we should think about a house before...Dominic?"

He tightened his hand around hers. Definitely one lucky son of a bitch. "How do you feel about London?"

"I've never been there."

"I'll take you. How soon...will they release me?"

"Not until you can have a conversation without gasping in pain."

"Which is why it's time for you to go, Rebecca," a voice said from the doorway.

Dominic opened his eyes. He glanced over, his joy fading to irritation. "What are you doing here?"

Nathan advanced further into the room. "I'm your doctor."

"Tell me he didn't—"

"Save your life? Yeah, that would be me." There was no mistaking the smugness in his voice.

"Arrogant prick," Dom muttered.

The arrogant prick smiled.

"I want a new doctor."

"I don't blame you, but she can't do it."

"Why not?"

"Because she's so caught up in the fact that you're alive she's failed to see just how much her presence is hurting you." He glanced at Rebecca before settling his gaze back on Dom. "On a scale of one to ten, where would you put your level of pain, twelve?"

Rebecca looked closer at him. "Jesus, Dom."

"And the doctor returns," the prick stated sarcastically. "Go home, Rebecca, get some rest. You look nearly as bad as my patient."

As she stood to move away, Dominic reached for her, "Wait." He gasped, unable to catch his breath as pain snaked throughout his entire body.

"Stubborn bastard," the prick muttered.

"Bloody wanker," Dom fired back. Too bad it didn't have the bite he'd been going for as he couldn't seem to catch his breath.

"Dominic?"

"Rebecca," the prick warned.

"Just give us a damn minute, will you?" Dom managed, never taking his gaze off Becca. "There's something we need to clear up."

"What?" she asked.

"Us."

Her gaze left his to look at Nathan, then returned. "Don't worry about him," Dominic stated. "He's not important."

"No, I'm just the man who stopped you from bleeding out on the emergency room floor. Then patched you back together."

"And you call me arrogant," Dom muttered. Slowly, he took hold of Rebecca's hand once again. "Just so we're clear, you'll marry me?"

"Is your flat in London big enough for me, five kids, a dog and a minivan?"

He thought of the tiny little place he never spent much time in. "Yes, no, what breed and no way in hell are we ever getting a mini...did you say five?"

"Yes."

He couldn't disguise the note of panic in his voice. "You want to drag five kids around the world with us? Through the tours and—"

"Yes," she said without hesitation, a broad smile in place.

He just looked at her for a moment while his heart raced and he broke into a sweat. *Jesus.* Before her he'd never imagined himself with one child, let along five.

"Did you know your heart rate does a very interesting two-step whenever I say 'kids'?"

"Does it? Maybe it's a number thing. How about three? Three's a good number."

"I want a big family, Dominic. With you." Her smile blinded. "There goes your heart rate again."

The future stretched out before him. The thought of her growing large with child, *his* child, had warmth spreading inside of him. And maybe a touch of fear. "As long as one looks like you."

"Genetically speaking, the chances of that are slim."

"I'll make it happen."

"I believe you would."

He smiled.

She laughed. Then kissed him on the mouth. "Yes, I'll marry you."

Thank God. He tightened his hand around hers as his eyes drifted closed.

"One more thing."

Uh-oh. He opened his eyes with difficulty.

"I think we should find a home closer to Noah and Isabeau. That way our kids can grow up together."

There it was again, that warm feeling in his stomach. "Sure."

"That was too easy. I thought you hated California?"

It's where his family was. Truthfully, where he always wanted to be. He was tired of circling the globe looking for something that had been right here the whole time.

Her eyes softened and she kissed him again. "I love you, Dominic. I've never stopped."

"I love you, Dominic."

He looked in her eyes, those gorgeous emerald eyes and said what he should have said years ago. "I love you." The words slipped out so natural and right that he said them again. "I love you, Rebecca."

Coming soon...

WRECKED
Blind Man's Alibi #1

She was destined to show him the joy and pain of living.

Joe Campbell has it all: money, success, and fame. As lead singer of alternative rock band Blind Man's Alibi, he holds the vague conviction that life on the road, and nights filled with meaningless sexual encounters, is enough. Until her – Emma Travers. She is a breath of fresh air. Sunshine to his darkness. The one who changes him, pushes him, and teaches him to truly live. He never imagines she is hiding a devastating secret. Or that the same emotion that could steal his heart, would ultimately break it.

Please turn the page for a preview

Chapter One

April 3

"Sorry, but sucking off a narcissistic asshole who's so damn drunk he can't recall the words to his own song is not my idea of a good time."

His bark of laughter echoed in the empty hall. "You really are a ray of sunshine, aren't you?"

God, what a terrible idea this had been. Hoping to put some distance between them, Emma Travers quickened her pace, only to stumble over the uncustomary height of the heels her best friend Alison had convinced her to wear. Her ankle screamed in protest, forcing her to skid to a halt. Balancing precariously so she didn't face plant on the concrete, she struggled against the zippers, finally succeeding in pulling the rhinestone studded stilettoes from her swollen feet. She barely resisted the urge to turn around and throw them at the head of the man who'd pissed her off faster than a Bugatti Veyron went zero to sixty, and instead tossed them aside and continued her escape in bare feet.

"Come back and see me sometime, Emma," Joe Campbell, lead singer of the British alternative metal band *Blind Man's Alibi*, called out to her.

Fat chance!

"I could use a bit of sunshine in my life." The murmur hit her ears like a shout, and stopped her in her tracks.

Well, shit.

Emma remained rooted in place, unable to decide if he was for real, or filling her with pretty words in order to get her to stay and sleep with him. He sounded sincere enough, but the only way to know for certain was to face him. Something she really did not want to do.

Not that he was painful to look at. Oh no, Joe Campbell was extremely pleasing to the eye, a fact he knew too well. One, she was certain, he used to his advantage whenever an occasion presented itself. Like tonight, when she'd gone against character and accepted his invitation backstage after the show.

One glimpse of the man who stood alone in the room she'd been unceremoniously delivered to and Emma went hot all over. Unable to speak she'd allowed her gaze to take a long, slow journey over his body. His torso was bare, giving her an unobstructed view of hardened pecs, a flat washboard stomach and muscles that rippled and shifted making the Chinese dragon that wrapped around his left upper arm and onto his chest seem alive as he slipped his left hand into the front pocket of his jeans. Dear God those jeans! The way they hung on his lean hips, the top button undone like he'd just pulled them on. They rode so low there was no mistaking that underneath them he was commando. Her gaze had locked on the obvious bulge behind his fly and for a moment, she'd actually considered dropping to her knees before him and taking a taste.

Then he'd opened his mouth. What was that saying? He'd managed to take the wind out of her sails.

With a deep breath for courage, Emma turned around and was greeted by the same image of the man as before. Except that the whiskey bottle he'd held in his right hand and lifted to those delectable lips too many times to count, was nowhere to be seen. Oh great, and the hulking brute who'd brought her backstage, stood leaning against the wall to Joe's right.

Gary, she was pretty certain he'd introduced himself as Gary, held his arms crossed before him, head tipped toward the floor in a pseudo relaxed pose designed to give the impression he hadn't just heard every damn word they'd said. He blew the image to shit when he lifted his head and winked at her. Winked! Was everyone in the music industry completely bonkers?

Emma did her best to ignore the brute and focused on the singer. "You're a real piece of work, you know that?"

"What did you expect?"

Good question.

"I guess I hoped the stage show was just

that, a show, and that there was a decent guy behind all of that. Maybe I wanted to believe the 'I'm too sexy for my own good' attitude was just publicity."

"Sorry to disappoint," he said in a tone that didn't sound regretful at all. He strode toward her, his long legs closing the distance in half the time it had taken her to get this far. She made herself stand her ground as he stepped in close, closer than she'd yet allowed him to get. Close enough she caught the subtle hint of soap on his skin, and whiskey on his breath. "You're right about one thing, I'm an asshole. But it wasn't the alcohol that caused me to lose my words tonight, Emma Travers. It was you."

His chin-length brown hair was nearly dry now and hung over his eyes as if windblown, though nary a wisp of air blew from the vents above. Eyes she was surprised to learn were two different colors – one brown, the other a mix of brown and green. "You excel at telling a girl what she wants to hear, I'll give you that."

His gaze didn't flinch. "How can you doubt the truth? You were there, close enough to touch me." His voice dropped an octave. "All you had to do was reach out."

An image of hands pawing and clutching at him whenever he'd trekked too close to the edge of the stage flashed through her mind. "Is that what you wanted me to do? Grope you like the other women in the audience. Do you actually enjoy that?"

He suddenly appeared to have a bad taste in his mouth. "Not particularly."

"Yet you expect me to believe that for some unknown reason you wanted me to touch you?"

"You stood out from the crowd. Not singing, not screaming, just standing in the front row. It was impossible not to notice you. I wondered why you were at the show; you didn't seem to be having a good time. Then you smiled at me...my mind blanked."

What the hell was she supposed to say to that? Thanks for noticing me?

"I was feeding you lines and you just stood there, staring." Much the same way as she was doing now. Christ he was beautiful. Her fingers itched with the need to trace his lips, his mustache, the little hairless spots on the outside of his bottom lip and that sexy as hell strip of facial hair that went from the center of his full lower lip down, to blend into his short trimmed beard. Her throat went dry as dust, making it hard to swallow. "So why me? I'm not actually supposed to believe you saw me and lost your words, am I?"

"That's what happened." he stated matter-of-factly. "You know it's true, you were there."

Emma shook her head.

"Contrary to what you think, I was not too drunk to remember the lyrics. You see, I'm an accomplished drinker. I've been at it a long time. Long enough to know that forgetting the words to one of my songs is about as never-going-to-happen as forgetting how to please a woman."

"Why?"

"Why what, Sunshine?"

"Why are you a practiced drunk? Is that all you do, spend your free time partying?"

"Interesting. You don't question my forgetting how to please a woman?"

"Hah! You could probably pull that off if you were comatose."

The corners of his mouth kicked up into a smile. His eyes blazed with arrogance. Slowly, ever so slowly his right hand lifted toward her face.

The calloused tips of his fingers glanced off her cheek as she caught his wrist. "It's time for me to go."

"Stay." His deep voice combined with his intent gaze spread warmth throughout her body.

She forced herself to look away. Her eyes trailed a path down his right arm, over the bulge of bicep, the bend of his elbow, to where her hand circled his wrist. Beneath her thumb, which was busy making slow, gentle sweeps across his skin – *When exactly had it started doing that?* – a tattoo drew her attention. Measures of music circled his wrist once, twice, three times before ending in a large, red and black abstract G clef on the outside of his forearm.

"Tell me why you came backstage to find me if you weren't interested in, how did you put it, 'Sucking off a narcissistic asshole'?"

She felt bad for about ten seconds, then recalled the insulting way he'd treated her when first she'd entered his room.

"Why did you come backstage, Em?"

Shock? Curiosity? Because she couldn't wrap her mind around why someone like him would choose someone like her?

Emma wasn't sure if that was what he wanted to hear. She was certain he wasn't interested in knowing that ever since the day her oncologist informed her there was nothing more that could be done, she swore to pack as much living as she could into the time she had left. To squeeze every last drop of juice out of life.

She kept all of that to herself, instead releasing him and taking a step beck. With a deep breath to center herself she met his gaze. "I'll stay."

He flashed her a crooked smile.

"But no more alcohol."

"Done." He turned and motioned toward the room in a way that told her she was to take the lead.

Emma snatched her shoes off the floor. As she skirted around the man who made panties drop around the globe she told him, "Just so you know, I'm not sleeping with you, no matter how many pretty words you throw my way."

"You keep telling yourself that, Sunshine. Maybe you'll even begin to believe it."

A Note from Sarah

Thank you so much for reading **Midnight Heat**. I do hope that if you liked the story, that you would please leave a review. Not only does a review help spread the word to other readers, it allows authors to learn whether you'd like to see more stories like this from us. I love hearing from readers and talking to them whenever I can. You can always drop me an email at sarah@sarahgrimm.com

If you'd like to stay up to date with me and what's coming next you can sign up for my newsletter at www.sarahgrimm.com where you can also find links to my Facebook Page, my Black Phoenix Reader Group, and my Street Team.

Thanks again for reading my book. You are the reason I get to do what I do.

About the Author

As a young girl **Sarah Grimm** always had a story to tell. At times they were funny, other times scary, but they always ended with a happily-ever-after. Sarah spent years scribbling in notebooks, filling the pages with partial chapters and the margins with titles and story ideas. She told friends the characters spoke to her, and that she was compelled to get their stories on paper. Eventually, she sat down at a computer and wrote her first tale of dangerously sexy suspense.

Sarah lives in West Michigan with her husband, two sons, and three rescue dogs. Between mom's taxi service, her day job, and keeping the books for the family marine repair business, Sarah can be found curled in her favorite chair, crafting her next novel. Visit her online at http://www.sarahgrimm.com

Other Books by Sarah Grimm